In Grandma's Room

Creepy Little

Nightmares

Horror for the whole family.

Chapter

1

Ashley Rice assumed he was still asleep or was imagining things. Either was possible considering the circumstances. Right now, he was tucked up in bed, the Spider-Man lampshade giving off a soft orange glow, because regardless of whether he was imagining things or not, he liked the light left on at night. It made him feel safer, although as to why he wasn't entirely clear. If pressed, he would say it was because he could then see anything that happened to come for him, be it a ten-foot monster or a tiny spider crawling across his face. Both possibilities were equally terrifying.

But what he was hearing now wasn't coming from inside his room or outside, running sharp claws across the window, but in the empty bedroom next to his. It had been empty for a few weeks now and no one was allowed in there. In fact, as far as he was aware it was only his mother, Rebecca, who had a key to get in, and she kept it hidden. And she *never* went in there.

There, it came again. What sounded like a thud, as if someone had dropped something heavy or had punched the wall. It made him flinch, jerk like he'd been slapped. It also made his heart thud harder in his chest as if imitating the thudding next door. It had happened four or five times now and it was starting to really freak him out. He had never gone in that room before because it smelled bad and gave him the creeps, so he had no idea what was actually kept in there now. Surely there wasn't some kind of animal or bird that had somehow found a way in through an open window? He really ought to check. Be brave, so that he could tell his younger brother, Karl, tomorrow that he'd actually gone in there. It wouldn't be the complete truth, of course, because he didn't have the key, but Karl didn't need to know that.

Karl was already in awe of his big brother for sticking up for him when that bully, Robert, tried to push him off the swing the other day. Robert was bigger than Ashley, but that hadn't stopped him. Robert hadn't touched Karl since, and Ashley was glad about that. So, if tomorrow he told him he'd gone to check the noises he'd heard in *that* room, the kid would think him a god. He'd do anything he asked of him, like beg Mum to buy more of those awesome, yet expensive chocolate biscuits he liked so much that she only bought at Christmas. Karl was good at that, putting on his best sorrowful, pleading look. Mum fell for it every time. When Ashley had been eight, like his brother was now, it had never worked. That wasn't fair.

He jumped when another, louder thud sounded, but this time on the wall separating his and the spare room. Then, what he thought might have been whispering or soft chuckling. Or cackling, more to the point. Suddenly, he wasn't feeling so brave anymore. Suddenly, his stomach felt as though he'd eaten too much chocolate again and was going to throw up.

Ashley considered his limited options. He could try and ignore it and go back to sleep, because the possibility he was dreaming was now overruled. But the chances of this happening were extremely limited. He was too awake now, and his heart was too heavy in his chest. He could run downstairs and tell his parents, who were watching something on TV, but they would tell him to get back to bed. *It's late and you got school tomorrow, for God's sake.* Or he could go and check it out, which had been his original plan.

It might even be Karl who had somehow found the key and sneaked in. Just lately, since the room became empty, Ashley had caught him several times trying the doorhandle in the hope their mum had forgotten to lock it. He said he had left a toy in there a couple of weeks ago and wanted it back. Mum said she would buy him a new one but kept forgetting. But why not just go in there and get it for him?

The cackling returned. Muffled as though with a hand over their mouth, trying not to be heard.

Maybe whoever it was thought Ashley was asleep and was prancing about in there in complete privacy. Or what if it was Karl trying to scare him? Wouldn't be the first time with his childish games.

That did it.

Ashley climbed out of bed and crept towards his bedroom door. As quietly as he could, he opened it and stepped outside. The room was to his left and the door was closed. If it was Karl in there, he was going to wet himself when Ashley threw the door wide open. They were strictly prohibited from even trying to go in, but that didn't always work when it came to inquisitive kids. The temptation was too much, and Karl was as curious as anyone he'd ever met.

Before seeing if it was open or not, he put his ear to the door, a grin on his face now. He imagined Karl jumping about on the bed, no doubt laughing himself. He wondered what their mum would say if she caught him in there. Karl would be grounded for a month. Then a shuffling sound came. Something heavy being dragged along the floor it seemed.

Ashley took a deep breath and made to swing the door wide open.

It was locked.

He tried again. A lock had been fitted to the door handle a short time ago and the door wouldn't budge. Faint chuckling or whispering came from in there again. So if it was locked, who was in there? As an afterthought, he went to his brother's room and quietly opened the door. Karl lay there in bed, fast asleep. Now Ashley wasn't grinning.

He closed the door again and listened in to the supposedly empty room.

"Ashley!" came a sharp bark from behind the door, almost making him trip over his feet as he staggered back.

Instead of answering, he ran back to his own room, closed the door and jumped into bed, covering himself with the blankets. This was wrong, all wrong. Impossibly wrong. Because the voice that had barked his name sounded very similar to his grandma, Edna. But she had died two weeks ago in that very room, and no one had been allowed in since.

Chapter

2

Ashley awoke to mother opening the curtains. The sun was shining in, so bright it might have been directly outside his window.

"Wakey-wakey, sleepy. Time for school."

"Aww, do I have to? I wanna sleep a bit longer."

"Nope. You can sleep in at the weekends. Up!" She threw back the blankets and tickled his ribs, causing him to squirm and giggle.

"Stop! What about Karl? He's still asleep."

"He's downstairs eating breakfast. Yours, by the way, is getting cold already, so move!"

Ashley groaned and sat up, his mother watching as she left to make sure he really did get up. Sometimes, if he waited until she went back downstairs, he could sneak in an extra five minutes. And weren't those extra five minutes better than a whole night's sleep sometimes?

"Up!" she called from the top of the stairs.

"I'm comin'!"

Dammit. Didn't work.

He swung his legs out of bed, groaning about having to get up so early, how he hated school and wished he was a grown up so he didn't have to anymore. This was all a lie, though, and deep down he knew it. Once he got to school, all thoughts of being sleepy and tired and a grown-up vanished as quickly as his annoyance at being rudely awoken. Still wasn't fair, though.

He dressed and headed towards the stairs, then stopped. A nagging doubt in his mind that had caused him to halt. Something happened last night and he couldn't quite remember what, like a lingering dream slowly fading away. He stuck his head in Karl's room to see if he really was up or not—again, wouldn't be the first time his mother had lied to him—saw that he was and made to go downstairs again.

Then he remembered.

It all came flooding back like a sugar rush to the head. The thuds, something being dragged then his name mentioned that sounded ominously like Grandma.

A chill rippled through him as though a cold gust of wind had suddenly blown past. Surely it had been a dream, though, right? Had to have been. He had gone to Grandma's funeral with the rest of the family. Admittedly, they had been the only ones to go, but he had definitely gone. Had even seen the body lowered.

He had thought it a little strange that Mum hadn't cried. At all. Mum was Grandma's daughter, so yeah, okay, Grandma was really weird at the end, acting strange, but even so, she should have at least cried a little, shouldn't she? And when his parents had come afterwards, Mum had looked relieved, even. As though something bad that had been worrying her had suddenly been lifted. She had poured herself a large glass of wine and smiled as she drank it. So had Dad. He had heard them whispering, then Dad had kissed her and gave her a hug. Adults were weird.

Inside Grandma's room was quiet now as he pressed his ear to the door. Thinking about it, there was no way he had been dreaming. The recollection was too vivid. He could almost feel the way his heart had pounded in his chest, the sharp intake of air when his name was mentioned. But now, with the sun beaming its golden rays at him, birds singing outside, things seemed different.

Nope, it was definitely silent in there. He tried the door. Obviously locked as it always had been. Regardless, he would ask her why.. It *demanded* to be asked about.

When he walked into the kitchen, Karl was playing around with his food, making stupid burping noises. Ashley slapped him on the back of the head.

"Oww!"

"Still making baby sounds? Mum changed your nappy yet?"

"I ain't no baby. You're a baby. I heard you crying last night. Like a little baby. Probably wet the bed, as well."

"Kids, behave!" called out their mother.

Ashley couldn't even respond or retaliate. *Crying*? Under normal circumstances, he might have pulled his brother's curly, blond hair from behind, or perhaps flicked his ear, twisted a nipple even. After what happened last night and remembering how scared he had been, it was totally feasible he had cried. Even in his sleep. That seemingly innocent taunt by Karl shocked him more than Karl could ever have wished for.

He sat at the table and took a bite of his toast, not really feeling that hungry at all. He tried to replay everything that happened once more, get his story right before he made a fool of himself. Yes, he had definitely been awake.

"Mum?"

"Yes? What now?"

He turned to look at her as she washed dishes in the sink. He thought she looked younger now, for some reason, as if that great weight that had been on her shoulders since Grandma died had also given her back ten years of her life. Her shoulder-length brown hair was now perfect, not a strand missing. When Grandma lived with them, it was often straggly, like she'd just woken up. Like Ashley's—same colour, slightly shorter, but always a corkscrew here and there that refused to behave. There had been wrinkles around her sharp, green eyes that were now gone, and he could have sworn she had lost weight.

She had started humming to herself as she went about doing the household chores. Before, she had been quiet, snapped at the slightest thing, arguing with Dad. Had always been nervous around Grandma. Earlier, he hadn't wanted to become a grown-up ever, preferring to remain as a twelve-year-old forever. But now it looked so much easier. Seeing her smile, the twinkle in her eyes, hugs and kisses now once more a habit rather than a rarity, his thoughts on that had changed. Being an adult seemed pretty cool. Even Dad, who had been short-tempered and prone to disappearing to the pub on regular occasions after work, was here more often, cuddling up to Mum on the sofa again. Gross, but still pretty cool.

"Mum, umm…last night, I heard noises coming from Grandma's room. And I wasn't asleep and imagining things, if that's what you're thinking. I got up to check, thinking it was Karl in there."

Suddenly, there was silence. As if time had stopped altogether. Even Karl was frozen, a piece of toast dangling from his fingers mid-air, eyes bulging, staring at his brother as though he had gone mad. There might have been a flicker of unease in his eyes, too. Could he have heard the same thing but been too scared to mention it? Mum was also frozen, her back to him but her hands holding a dish in the air. Were her hands shaking? It stayed this way for a few seconds, Karl glaring at Ashley, Mum a statue, while the water continued running into the sink, water and soap suds running down her wrists.

It was his mother who reacted first. The dish slipped from her hand and crashed onto the floor, smashing into dozens of pieces. In the relative silence it had sounded like a bomb had exploded. Blood ran down her fingers from a small gash.

"Darn!" she hissed. "Now look what you made me do!"

"But, I—"

"What on earth are you talking about, Ashley? You're scaring your brother. Don't you say things like that. You were dreaming. Of course, you were dreaming!"

"But I wasn't. I got up thinking it was Karl in there, like someone had unlocked the door and left it open. I heard thudding and shuffling and then someone said my na—"

"Ashley Rice, you be quiet now! Do you hear me? Don't you dare talk about things like that. The room is empty, and no one goes in there except me. You were dreaming. Now finish your breakfast and get ready for school."

"But I don't understand. Why do you keep the room locked if there's nothing in there? Grandma's dead so what difference does it ma—"

"Shut up! Go get dressed. Now!"

Ashley was shocked. He had never heard her yell that loudly. Not even when he or Karl were fighting or one of them broke something accidently. A few months ago, they had been tussling on their parents' bed and had inadvertently knocked over the bedside lamp and broke it. Apparently, it had been a present or something, yet even then she hadn't screamed at them as loudly.

He looked to Karl who looked on the verge of tears, his piece of toast still dangling there, forgotten. Not daring to continue insisting, Ashley rose from his chair and stormed off, while his mother cursed under her breath scooping up the broken plate.

He began to cry. There was a tone in his mother's voice that sounded alien, as though it belonged to another. She never swore in front of the kids, either. That was one of her unbroken laws, and it annoyed the hell out of her if they were watching a movie together as a family and there was swearing. According to which movie, perhaps an action or mild horror one, sometimes she'd watch it first just to make sure there wasn't any profanity. Especially if Karl would be watching it as well.

Ashley sat on his bed, sobbing quietly, feeling sorry for himself and not understanding the sudden outburst. He'd only asked a question. It wasn't as if *he'd* sworn or said or done something bad. Dejectedly, he began to get dressed, knowing that if he was late for school, she'd scream at him again given her current mood. He heard Karl creeping up the stairs to get ready as well, so he waited for Karl to come bursting into his room and ask him what the hell that was all about. But that didn't happen. Maybe he was also too scared. Even little brothers knew when it was best to keep one's mouth shut.

Ashley finished dressing and left the bedroom to go clean his teeth before leaving. As he passed Grandma's old room, he paused. Goosebumps rose on his arm, and the hair on the back of his neck prickled. He wasn't completely sure, but he was pretty certain he had just seen a shadow move under the door and heard a faint cackle.

Chapter

3

Edna's Story

Candle lights flickered briefly in the dark room then settled down again, causing a nervous chuckle to emanate around the people sitting at the round table. Probably a rogue gust of wind from an open window somewhere or the fireplace. There were six of them, glancing each other's way, nervous smiles on some, twitches on the lips of others barely able to contain the giggle that threatened to ruin the moment. All of them were either nervous or on the verge of laughter. All of them except Edna's husband, Richard, who looked as serious as he always did. He had barely smiled when his first daughter, Alison, was born, and even less, when Edna announced she was pregnant again. The baby inside her kicked lightly as though reminding her she was still there and the atmosphere in the room made her uneasy, as well. As though she could sense even from the warm confines of the womb what was taking place.

Edna rubbed a hand over her protruding belly. *Don't you worry, Rebecca. Mother's here. She won't let anything happen to you.* Somehow, she knew it would be another girl.

Alison was upstairs, fast asleep. Four years old and as beautiful as anything God had conceived on Earth. Even more so. Long black hair as smooth as silk, green eyes like sparkling jewels, and a contagious, radiant smile, like a rainbow. Didn't matter that her father didn't quite see things this way. Didn't matter that he yelled at Edna to stop the bloody girl from crying or God help me… Didn't matter. He would never dare put a hand on her beloved daughter. She would kill anyone that tried to hurt her little baby.

The aging woman sitting beside Richard appeared deadly serious as though what she was about to attempt was dangerous. Life-threatening. She glared when one of the women sitting at the table did giggle.

"Quiet!" hissed the old woman—Mary might have been her name.

Edna wasn't sure. All she knew was that she didn't want this woman—or any of these people, for that matter—in her home. But as Richard liked to remind her at every opportunity, he was the bread winner in this family. Thus, he could do whatever the hell he pleased when in it. She couldn't argue that, much as she would have liked to. Edna wasn't entirely sure what he did for a living, but it involved a lot of travelling, a lot of money passing hands. It meant they could live in this huge house with its nine bedrooms, seven bathrooms, and so many other rooms. She didn't think she'd even been in them all. She knew he made most of his money just after the Second World War ended just five years earlier, but she wouldn't dream of questioning him about it. Sufficed to say, they lived with more than enough, that they should never worry about a single thing again.

Except for this.

Edna stood at the back of the room, refusing to sit with them while they held hands and the candles flickered. At the slightest sign of distress, she would leave them to their morbid games and drunken fun.

The room was silent once again, only their breathing to be heard.

"Dorothy Edwards, are you here with us?" said Mary in a loud, confident voice.

Eyes flickered in all directions, as though searching for the mysterious and enigmatic woman.

"Dorothy, if you are here, please give us a sign."

Edna watched Richard, his eyes virtually bulging from their sockets, barely breathing. This charade meant so much to him. Why, she couldn't understand. He had the perfect life. What was the interest in the afterlife?

A flame flickered and snuffed out. Tiny gasps came from the two women sitting at the table. A log cracked like a whip in the fireplace, making them all jump.

"I know you're here, Dorothy. I can sense your presence. Let the others know of your presence, too. I implore you."

The heavy, crimson curtains twitched, as though someone was hiding behind them. Maybe there was. This was, after all, a charade, wasn't it? When people died, as far as Edna was concerned, they stayed that way. There was no such thing as ghosts. It was the work of charlatans, those seeking to earn a few pennies at the expense of others' debility and suffering. They should be put in prison. Just like this Mary.

Another of the six candles flickered and puffed out. The air seemed to grow heavier, stuffier, as if the fireplace was letting out too much smoke. But the smoke that Edna saw was rising straight up the chimney.

"I feel you, Dorothy. Let us know you are here with us. There is someone who would like to speak with you."

The curtains twitched again. At any second, Edna expected to see a human shape form behind them, perhaps wave briefly then disappear. The actor escaping through one of the many secret doors and passageways. Instead, the room darkened, as if some great shadow had slowly dropped down from the ceiling. The temperature fell with it and Edna felt goosebumps prickle her skin. Whether from nerves or the sudden cold, she didn't know. Everyone was looking around the room now, no one smirking or giggling anymore.

"Reveal yourself to us, Dorothy. Show you are still with us."

Richard's face was red, as though he had stopped breathing. Eyes bulging still, barely daring to move. Then, a fine mist, like a dissipating fog, swirled in the far corner by the curtains. One moment, it was long and elongated, then, the next, it was short and round like a cloud. What sounded like a groan, weak and sorrowful, accompanied it. Edna wrapped her hands across her stomach as though trying to protect her unborn child from unwelcome forces.

The mist grew thicker, still swirling, particles of dust floating and glittering like distant stars. Two of those particles grew larger, until they were the size of marbles, like what Edna used to play with as a child. And she gasped, like everyone else, when she realised they were eyes. They moved from side to side, tiny and gleaming like fireballs, taking in the sight before them, Edna in the far corner. The groaning grew louder, now almost like a faraway wail. The mist took on a thicker, more dense aspect, and slowly the shape of a human grew, grey and featureless, except those eyes.

"Welcome, Dorothy. There's no need to be scared. We're all here to help you. You can trust us. Can you speak with us?"

Edna wanted to speak for her. This was an aberration, a trick; it had to be. Edna wanted to scream at it to go away. Whatever repugnant, scandalous prank this woman was playing on them had to stop. Yet, she knew if she said something, Richard would be furious. He would have no qualms about using his hands on her later, regardless of the baby inside her. It wouldn't be the first time. Richard right now looked enthralled as he glared at the so-called spirit. Even though it had taken on a more substantial appearance, Edna could still see the curtains through it, rippling slightly.

There were quiet murmurs from those present, all eyes wide and bulging, jaws dropped, hands clutching hands tighter than before.

"You are Dorothy Edwards, correct? You died in this house as a servant, six months ago? If so, one knock for yes, two for no."

A thud sounded on the table, making them all jump. Dorothy Edwards had worked for them until six months ago, when she fell down the stairs to the basement and broke her neck. After the funeral, Richard had started speaking of trying to make contact with her. Despite the hazy appearance, it certainly did look like her, long grey hair flowing behind it as though underwater. It was the right height as well, however impossible. It was a trick Mary had orchestrated to take Richard's money. Everyone wanted Richard's money, and he was too naïve and stupid to see through their falsities.

"You died from a heart attack, Dorothy?"

Two thuds.

"You were ill, with disease?"

Two thuds.

"You tripped and fell?"

One thud. The murmurs grew in crescendo, everyone looking at each other, Mary looking smug with herself.

A simple trick, thought Edna. *Give the actress the right information and just play along with it. How naïve, all of them.*

"And why are you still here, Dorothy? Can you not move on to your final resting place?"

Two thuds.

"Is there something you need to do? You have unfinished business?"

One thud.

"Is it something to do with this house? Richard wanted to contact you. He wanted to say he was sorry for what happened."

One thud.

"Y-yes, Dorothy. I'm sorry about the accident. I feel so bad, as though it was my fault. I just want you to know that. I gave money to your husband to take care of your child. Can…can you go to Heaven if you want to? Does it exist? Does Heaven exist?"

One thud. Two. Then a pounding as if a dozen fists were smashing the table. It rocked back and forth, splintering in the middle. One of the candles shot across the room. A woman was thrown from her chair, screaming as she banged her head on the thick rug. From some indeterminable place came another scream long and winded, of someone in extreme agony and distress. It seemed to come from all around them, above, below, from outside, from right next to them. A thousand lost souls wailing for help.

The people at the table all jumped up except Mary who remained seated, looking around in shock, while the woman knocked to the floor pulled herself to her feet. Richard was stunned too, his face pallid, looking like he didn't understand anything.

"Dorothy! Dorothy, calm down! We're your friends. Tell us what is wrong so we can help!"

The pounding continued, louder than before, as though someone was beating a drum in the room. The screaming intensified causing everyone, including Mary, to cover their ears.

"Is there something wrong, Dorothy? Is it something that happened before you died?"

Suddenly, silence. A single thud, and then everything was still and quiet again, except for the heavy panting from the guests. Edna had been about to run from the room, to Alison, who had surely awoken to such a scandalous racket.

"Is there a way you can tell or show us?"

No reply came, but Edna noticed the way Richard was looking nervous, twiddling his tie. Was she missing something?

"Is it the way you died, Dorothy? Did you not die the way we thought?"

And then total chaos ensued once more. The thudding was deafening. Loud banging came from the walls, on the ceiling, causing the plaster to crack. The lightbulb swung back and forth, almost smashing into the ceiling. It even came from beneath them, as if some huge creature was under the floorboards, punching and kicking its way through. Howls and wails reverberated as though they were immersed in some tragic, terrible catastrophe and everyone was dying around them, just like when the bombs fell from German planes only a few years earlier. The table they had been seated at flew across the room and crashed against the wall, sending hundreds of tiny splinters like shrapnel over their heads. Everyone ducked and covered their heads, this time including Mary.

The medium was trying to say something to Dorothy, but it was impossible for Edna to hear over the racket. A candle flew directly at Richard, hitting him in the side of the head, and then, immediately upon impact, silence returned once more.

No one dared to move, all still in shock about what they had just witnessed. They stayed where they were for a while, cowering against the wall or sprawled on the floor covering their heads. Only Richard remained standing, as if defying what he'd just seen. Then, sensing the spirit had gone, they all pulled themselves to their feet.

"What the hell just happened?" asked one of the guests. "Has this ever happened before, Mary?"

Mary looked visibly shaken as well, but slowly nodded. "Not all spirits are happy to be amongst us. Some hold grudges or feel there is something that needs to be said or done before they can move on. It seems to be the case with Dorothy. What could possibly be wrong with her, Richard?"

Richard shook his head, but he was smiling. "I have no idea, but that's not what's important right now. What is, is that we have proof of life after death."

He looked Edna's way, a big grin on his face like a spoiled child.

Disgusted, Edna turned and hurried off. It was hideous and disturbing, and she wanted no part of it.

Chapter

4

When bedtime came around that night, Ashley had all but forgotten about the incident in his grandma's room and the way his mother had acted at breakfast time. The day was too full of things to do for him to remember them anyway and bear any kind of grudge. There were football matches to be played, gossip to swap among friends, girls to annoy or, in some cases, admire. There were teachers to be wary and afraid of, far more than an angry mother. Some of the teachers liked to shout at the kids in front of the whole class, causing some to sob, which was highly embarrassing. It was one thing being yelled at by Mum or Dad at home; another entirely being yelled at in front of all his friends.

When he came home from school with Karl, there had been no mention of the earlier scene, anyway. And Mum was acting as though nothing had happened. She hugged and kissed them both, asked how their day had gone, what they had learned, and about homework. Everything was forgotten about.

Until now.

With Karl already in bed (it was a rule that Karl, being younger, had to be in bed by nine. Ashley had until ten), Ashley headed up the stairs to use the toilet and clean his teeth before getting into bed. There it was, that empty room, and everything came flooding back to him.

The door was closed as always, like a secret portal. After what happened last night and his mother's response this morning, it was as if the room held some terrible, huge secret—the lair to some terrifying monster that must never be allowed out.

After using the toilet, then brushing his teeth, he crept past the door, keeping as wide as berth as possible, in case it might suddenly be thrown open and some huge, hairy arm, with talons on the ends of its fingers to grab hold of him. Even so, he still strained to hear anything coming from within. Yet all was silent, only his thudding heart audible in his ears.

Quickly, he jumped into bed and pulled the blanket up as though it might offer protection against unwanted monsters. His dad would be up any second to kiss him goodnight, so he lay there patiently, unable to resist listening in to the room next door for any strange sounds. After what seemed an eternity, the thud of footsteps on the stairs told him his dad was coming to say goodnight.

"You good, kid?"

"Yeah, Dad."

"How was school today? Anything exciting? New girlfriend?"

"That's gross! I ain't never getting a girlfriend. Girls are stupid."

"That, son, is very true, but don't ever tell your mother I said that."

Ashley chuckled. He never got to see his dad as often as he would like. He worked doing something with numbers which sounded really boring, and he often worked until late. Something about having to make numbers meet for his clients so they didn't pay taxes, whatever that meant. And Dad was nothing like his mother. He never swore, and barely raised his voice. Sometimes Ashley thought Dad was scared of Mum; she was always telling him what to do, and he never argued back. And when Grandma died, Dad's relief had been visible for all to see. He often looked scared around her, too, seeming to avoid her as much as possible. Whenever Grandma had been in the living room, Dad had gone outside to mess around in the garden, or he sat at his laptop, claiming he was trying to write a book. When Grandma had been in her room, he never went in there, either, using any excuse not to have to take her medicine or supper to her. If Mum wasn't home for any reason, Dad would often forget on purpose. Not that it really mattered; Grandma had been pretty mad and senile in her last few years, anyway.

"Time for bed. Lights out." His Dad ruffled Ashley's hair and kissed him on the forehead.

Ashley thought of telling him about last night, then changed his mind. What was he going to say? Mum wouldn't give him the key, either.

His dad, Keith, turned off the light, leaving the orange glow of the lamp on. Ashley tried not to think about the empty room next door, or Grandma; instead, thinking about how he kind of liked Lindsey from his class and what he might say to her without blushing like an idiot and embarrassing himself. As he was trying to think of something witty and funny he soon drifted off.

He woke up some time later and could hear talking coming from outside his room. Still half asleep, his brain foggy, it sounded like two people arguing. He glanced at the Spider-Man clock on his wall—saw it was nearly three in the morning.

What the hell? Probably Mum and Dad again.

But then, as his brain slowly cleared away the foggy residue, he realised it wasn't his parents at all. And it wasn't coming from outside his room, either. It was coming from Grandma's room. He wasn't entirely sure, but it sounded pretty much like her, as well. He recognised that croaky, high-pitched voice. This time, though, it was darker, heavier, as if she was trying to impersonate a man. And the person she was apparently talking to was definitely a man. He had a voice that boomed like thunder.

Now fully awake, Ashley sat up and pressed an ear to the wall.

"Soon, very soon. It won't be long," the man said.

"But it's taking too long. I want it now!"

"Be patient. Such things require much patience and thought. One does not achieve such things in a single day."

"I want his body now." said the one in grandma's voice.

What might have been chuckling or coughing ensued, something foul and horrible that made Ashley's skin crawl and prickle as though being squeezed. What did that mean, 'I want his body'? Who was in there? Could he be dreaming again? He tugged on his earlobe hard, wincing at the pain. No, he was definitely awake.

A shuffling sound followed that caused the floorboards to creak, as if something heavy was being dragged across the room.

A thought, horrific and impossible at the same time, drifted through Ashley's mind. What if Grandma hadn't really died and Mum was keeping her locked up in there for some reason? What if they had buried someone else that day or the coffin had been empty?

But he had seen Grandma's bloated body in her bed the day she died. Well, not entirely, because Mum hadn't let him, but he had seen her lower body as curiosity got the better of him and he tried to peer in. It was only her face he hadn't seen, but that didn't matter; he would recognise her huge bulk and those horrible, flower dresses she wore anywhere.

It was quiet in the room again now, making him question once more whether he had really heard it. Nope. No way. He still had the goose bumps on his arms. The questions that had brushed past his mind as an afterthought were now at the forefront, demanding to be answered. Why would Mum do such a thing— keep her hidden? The more he thought about it, the more possible it seemed. Really, he ought to go and investigate, check to see if it was true or not. Mum dropping the plate on the floor that morning, the way she had screamed at him not to talk about such things…that was why, wasn't it? He had discovered her secret and she had been in shock.

His parents would be fast asleep by now, so Ashley slowly climbed out of bed and headed to his door, opening it carefully then peering out onto the landing. Nothing moved, nothing made any sound, so he tiptoed across the landing to his parents' room. He knew Mum kept the key in her drawer; he'd seen her put it there and tell both him and Karl very seriously that if she ever caught them taking it, there would be no PlayStation or anything for the rest of the year. That had been two weeks ago in May. She then told them that not only would they be grounded for the rest of the year, but that she would send them both off to her sister's house to stay for a month. This was the biggest threat she could ever come up with. Mum's sister wasn't really her sister; she just called her that for reasons Ashley didn't know or particularly care. But Aunt Caroline was really religious. Every time they went to visit, they had to pray before lunch, pray before dinner, pray when they went to bed. If anyone so much as whispered a naughty word, as Karl had once done, she would lock the offender in the basement and make them read the entire Bible out loud before they were allowed out again. It had taken Karl three hours and a lot of begging and tears before she let him out. Mum had said nothing to help him. Visiting Aunt Caroline for a month was not going to happen.

But now things were different.

It was worth the risk.

Mum had lied and he had to know why.

He thought he understood what having a heart attack was all about. His own was in his throat, firmly lodged there and throbbing like a thing possessed. He thought he might throw up at the fear of getting caught taking the key, but curiosity and determination kept him going. If he didn't check that room and see if Grandma was in there or not, he would die from that lack of knowledge alone. It would fester in his mind like a rotting thing until it drove him mad.

Carefully, as gently as he possibly could, he pulled down the doorhandle and eased the door open.

Fortunately, the door didn't creak like something out of a horror film as he pushed it wider. Then, listening carefully for the sound of their breathing, he got on his hands and knees and crawled into the room, then around the bed until he came to his mother's side.

Surely they could hear his heart beating and would wake up at any second? It was too late now, anyway. If one of them woke up now, it would look like he was either trying to find that key or grab some money from their trouser pockets, and both meant certain death. Or something very similar.

He reached the small bedside table with its three drawers and opened the bottom one. Inside was his mother's underwear, which was gross, but that was the least of his worries. He rummaged around, reaching right to the back until his fingers rested on something cold and metallic. Ashley picked it up, drew it from the drawer, and closed it again before returning outside.

Just as he was about to stand up, his mother mumbled something in her sleep, almost causing another possible heart attack. She absently rubbed her nose, mumbled something incoherent again, and resumed snoring gently.

Once outside, he felt an immense weight lifted from his shoulders, but the job wasn't done yet. He still had to return the key, after all, but first, and potentially more life-threatening, was to find out who, if anyone, was in that room.

Only, now that he had the key poised, he wasn't sure if he could go through with it. What might happen if he opened the door and Grandma was in there, starving to death perhaps, or drooling at the mouth and totally, utterly mad? She was already mad before she (supposedly) died, so what would she be like now, locked up in a room for the last two weeks? And if that was the case, how was she going to the toilet? Washing herself? Would she reach out and grab him, try to eat him? Smother him in all that blubber that made her look like an old, diseased walrus?

And what if there was nobody in there at all? That could mean he was going mad, as well. Hadn't he learned something at school the other day about madness being hereditary? There was a hospital for people like that nearby—Northgate Hospital for the Mentally Impaired. Grandma had been there several times.

Ashley didn't want to go mad. He'd seen films about that, where people drooled at the mouth and wet themselves, completely unaware. They wandered aimlessly back and forth in corridors or banged their heads against a wall, over and over. That was scary.

But it was too late now. He'd risked his life getting the key, so he might as well make it worthwhile.

He held the key up, aware that his hand was shaking, and slid the key into the lock. But just as he began to turn, there was a noise to his right. He grabbed the key and prepared to run, when the door to Karl's bedroom opened.

Karl stumbled out, rubbing his eyes and headed towards the toilet. He stopped before he reached it and turned around, frowning. "What are you doing?"

"Shut up!" hissed Ashley. "Go to the toilet and get back to bed."

"Wait. Are you going in there?"

"Ssh! You'll wake Mum."

"But are you or not? Mum will kill you. Why'd ya wanna go in? Is it 'cause of what you said yesterday?"

Darn. Karl was as stubborn as their mother. Unless he got answers, he would start the mind games, use this act of rebellion against him, use it as blackmail. Karl was very good at getting what he wanted.

"Yes, okay! I heard noises. I just want to know what or who is in there. Okay? Now go."

"I wanna see too."

"*No*! You're not coming in. Get to bed!"

"Then come morning I'll tell Mum that you went in. How'd you get the key, anyway? Where was it?"

He could have strangled him there and then. But if he did that, it would certainly wake their parents, and he still had to return the darn key.

"I just want to have a quick look, that's all. I thought you wanted to go to the toilet, anyway?"

"I don't anymore. I wanna see in there. Did you really hear Grandma the other night? 'Cause she's dead, so…"

He left the statement hanging, like a corpse from a noose, but he need not have finished. Ashley already knew the implied answer to his question. "I don't know. That's why I want to check. Maybe I was dreaming, maybe I wasn't. But I need to know."

"Okay, then. What you waiting for?"

"For you to go back to bed."

"Well, I'm not."

There was no point arguing the matter. The longer they stayed out here, the bigger the chance of one of their parents getting up, perhaps needing the toilet, as well. He hadn't thought of that and now little ripples of panic were fluttering his heart, teasing his stomach. He pretty much needed the toilet himself.

"Okay, but don't say a word, and stay there!"

Karl nodded, although from the sparkle in his eyes, Ashley thought there wasn't much chance of him waiting outside. And it also begged the question; what if there *was* someone in there? What if Grandma really was inside and when he opened the door, she came charging out after the pair of them? Ashley thought he might scream, but Karl definitely would. He'd scream and piss his pyjamas, maybe even die of fright. Was such a thing possible? Ashley thought it was.

He held up the key in a trembling hand and tried to insert it into the thin gap, needing to do so several times. His heart was a drum in his chest, beating manically, his lips very dry. Finally, he managed to insert it and slowly began to turn the key to the left.

Please don't be right behind the door, Grandma. Please.

There was a soft click as the door opened. Out here in the silence, it sounded like a bomb.

Ashley turned to glimpse at his brother, see if he looked as scared as Ashley felt. Absolutely, he did. Like he was going to scream at any second and go running to their parents' room. Ashley pushed the door open slightly further, just enough so one eye could peek in. Nothing moved inside, but a stuffy odour of mildew and dampness wafted out to greet him. Something else, too—like how Ashley sometimes smelled after he played football and needed a shower, his socks sweaty. Only this time it was a thousand times worse.

As though Grandma has been locked in there for weeks and hasn't showered.

Regardless, he pushed the door opened a little further—no backing out now. Karl was standing closer to him, trying to look in as well, both huddled close together as if trying to keep warm. Every slight movement from Karl made Ashley flinch. Ashley took a deep breath and prepared to step in the room.

"Just what the hell are you two doing?" came a hiss from behind them.

Simultaneously, Karl squealed and almost fell into the room in shock. Ashley jumped, gasped, and fell back, the door closing behind them, thus preventing Karl's fall. Ashley was pretty sure he had wet himself, while Karl most certainly had, judging from the small wet patch on the front of his pyjamas.

"How the hell did you get the key and what for? Are you two stupid? Mad? Your mother will kill the pair of you. *I* should as well."

"I…I just wanted to look. I heard noises the other night. It scared me. I wanted to see if Grandma was in there… If she was really dead or not."

"What the hell are you talking about, son? Of course, your grandmother is dead. Give me that key and get back to bed."

"S-sorry, Dad."

Ashley handed him the key. Both kids dashed off to their rooms and closed their doors. Now that Ashley was in bed, he really did need to go to the toilet, but was too scared to go back out there again in case his dad was there. If Dad told Mum what had just happened, the pair of them would be off to Aunt Caroline's for a month.

It was only pure and utter exhaustion that led to Ashley finally drifting off to sleep sometime later.

Chapter

5

When the kids came down for breakfast, the clue that something had happened or that something was wrong was in the silence. It was common among parents to joke that when the kids were noisy and misbehaving, it made them wonder why the hell they decided to have kids in the first place. That lack of any peace and quiet, if only for five minutes. Enough to drive one to drink or prescription drugs.

And yet, when the kids did actually act as the parents had been begging for, and there was some peace for a change, instead of embracing it, fear replaced it. Something had to be wrong with one of them. One of them was ill. Or had broken something and was too scared to admit it. Maybe one, or both, of them had done something at school and, as if by pretending they're not there, the parents wouldn't find out.

Normally, when they came down, it was usually one of them trying to get the other in trouble. A little tug on their hair, a sly kick under the table, flick a piece of cereal at the other's face. Even though Rebecca pretended she wasn't aware, she was more so than they could ever know. The giggles were the first sign. Then their voices raised. And shortly afterwards, the accusations began. Ashley said this... Karl did that... Ashley hit me... Karl kicked me... Until it got out of hand, as it always did, and she was forced to act as judge, jury, and executioner.

It didn't always seem so at the time, but having two children, who aside from their fighting actually took care of each other and acted as she had always hoped brothers would, made her happy and proud. She had grown up an only child after her sister, Alison, had died. She had always missed having someone at home to play with, share secrets that were meant for no parents. Then, when her dad died and she was left with just her mother, a broken figure, solitude and envy had become her sisters.

Her mother, who had just died two weeks ago—but there was no grief there, nothing but relief and a hope of finality—became a distant figure. Lost to grief and despondency, especially over losing Alison, Rebecca barely saw her mother anymore, except when absolutely necessary. Her smile had died when Alison did. Hope had left her when her husband, Richard, then died. She had become a recluse, locked behind a thousand windows and doors in that huge mansion. An eccentric. The Weirdo, as known by the kids when, on very rare occasions, she headed into town, always dressed in black, her face hidden behind a black veil, almost an embarrassment to her little daughter who still wasn't quite old enough to fully appreciate grief in all its dark glory.

It was mainly for this reason that Rebecca had a no-nonsense personality. Having to practically raise herself from an early age, she had little time for whingers and for those seemingly incapable of doing the slightest things on their own without help. It was also one of the main reasons she had found herself attracted to Keith—his determination to rise to the top in his chosen profession. She also made sure her kids were not spoiled and that if they wanted something, they had to earn it. Life wasn't easy, so get used to it— her favourite saying.

So when the kids came downstairs, quiet and timid, she saw in them the same things she saw in herself at roughly that age—worry and concern. Unease.

"You two are quiet today," she said in what she hoped was a jovial voice. "You okay?"

"Yeah," both said in unison

Both resumed eating their cereal in silence. One or both of them had done something; of that, she was positive. But what? Keith didn't have to work today, a rare day off, so he would be down soon. Maybe he knew. Maybe they'd broken something last night and were worried about her finding out. She knew their father was a lot more lenient with them—good cop, bad cop—so maybe he would have answers. They were both eating fine, so they couldn't be ill. Besides, both getting the flu or something at the exact same time was unlikely. So they had definitely broken something then. As soon as they left for school, it would be time to find out what. If it was the PlayStation, they'd be grounded for a week. That thing cost a fortune.

She tried not to show her combination of bemusement and concern as they finished their breakfast. Afterward, each rose and set their bowls in the sink, then headed upstairs. Now she was really worried. They *never* cleaned up after themselves.

As they got ready for school, Keith came down, his already thinning brown hair wild and tangled instead of the usual immaculate style. Sleep showed in his blue eyes, which he was rubbing. Day-old stubble stood out on his face. He looked ill, but she knew that was not the case. Besides, he was grinning. She was so used to seeing him in his dark suit, perfectly groomed as expected from an accountant. This, he liked to call his casual look, reserved only for his wife and kids on the rare days he didn't have to care about his appearance.

"Morning, dearest! Who's looking gorgeous, as always, this fine morning?"

"Well, obviously not you. You look like a tramp."

"Today, I am a tramp. I'm gonna sit in the garden drinking beer, slouching about and doing nothing. I don't even want to see anyone today."

"Good, because looking like that you won't. You'll scare them off." She kissed him and turned on the coffee machine.

"Kids gone to school already? It's quiet in here."

"No, they haven't. And for that precise reason, I want to speak to you when they've gone."

A look of suspicion appeared on his face, the slightest twitch in his eye, his smile briefly flickering. He knew something alright. She could read him like a book. After being married fourteen years, she knew everything about him. The same couldn't quite be said about her, but she had her reasons for keeping the odd secret close to her heart. Somewhere where nothing and nobody would ever trace it.

"Ah," he said. "Yeah, that."

"Yeah, that, what? They've broken something haven't they? I can tell when they're so quiet. Tell me they haven't broken the—"

"No, nothing like that. I wish it was just that. Last nig—" He stopped when footsteps thudded down the stairs.

She glanced at him, nervously, trying to read his thoughts, because now she was worried. If they hadn't broken anything then what was wrong?

"Hey, kiddos," he said. "Ready for school?"

Both shrugged and kissed their father. That neither of them looked him in the eyes wasn't lost on Rebecca either. They kissed her on the cheek too, again, not looking her in the eyes, and made a hasty and abrupt escape. As soon as the door closed, Rebecca turned to face her husband.

"Okay, what have they done? You said they haven't broken anything, but they've done something, so what is it?"

"Can I get my coffee first?"

"Oh, yeah."

She finished preparing his coffee, then gave it to him, and sat beside him at the breakfast table, her heart beating far too hard for her liking this early in the morning. She did not take her eyes off him. He knew better than to skirt around the issue.

He sighed. "I got up to go to the toilet last night, and I saw the kids outside on the landing."

"Yes, and?"

"Ashley had sneaked into our room while we were asleep, got the key to your mother's old room, and he was about to go in there. I caught him just as he opened the door."

Rebecca stared at him as though he'd just told her he wanted a divorce or some such impossibility. Her jaw dropped, eyes unblinking. A thousand different emotions collided with each other in her suddenly warped mind—rage, outrage, shock, disbelief. Keith was lying; he had to be. The kids knew they were strictly forbidden from going in there. Even talking about it, let alone trying to get in. There was a reason for it and that was why she had someone come and change the door handle, incorporating a lock into it. They knew better than that. She'd told them a thousand times what she would do if she caught them trying to get in. And now, apparently, they'd done so, anyway.

Then she remembered Ashley talking about hearing things coming from in there the other night. Her body froze as though an arctic wind had suddenly blown through the house, making her shiver involuntarily. Her stomach flipped, feeling like she would vomit if her stomach didn't calm itself down. Maybe she'd even have a heart attack.

Because this couldn't be happening.

"Did he actually go in the room? And don't lie."

"No. The door was open just a crack. When I came outside and asked them what the hell they were doing, they jumped and almost fell into the room, but not quite. It slammed shut instead."

"Where's the key?"

"I put it back in the drawer," said Keith

"Right, I'm gonna start carrying it with me from now on and putting it under the pillow at night. The little fool. He is in so much trouble when he gets home. No wonder he was so sheepish and quiet this morning. But Karl was in on it as well?"

"I don't know. He was standing behind his brother looking pretty scared to be honest. What's going on? Why the sudden interest in going in that room?"

Something Rebecca had dreaded since her mother died was what might be going on. She should have guessed it might happen. The signs were there, but it seemed such a crazy thing. It was an impossible situation.

So why did you have a lock fitted, then?

Because you knew all along, for years, that this was something that might, just might, occur. You've been preparing for it since you were a little girl. Just waiting for that day when...

When what? Rubbish! Ashley has been having nightmares, that's all. It's perfectly normal. All those horror films and games kids play these days, it wasn't surprising.

"Rebecca?"

"What?!" she snapped.

"I asked, why the sudden interest? Your mother's been dead for over two weeks."

How much could she really tell him about what she knew, or believed to know? Everything? Nothing? Surely, he deserved to know. He lived here, too. They were his children as much as hers. He'd seen the changes for himself and had been as terrified of his mother-in-law, like Rebecca had been. The whole family, in fact. But that was the thing...it was *her* secret to bear. *She* was the one who had grown up seeing the way her mother behaved, the things she did. The terrible things she said. It was her burden to carry. It was up to her to finish all this when the time came, and really, Keith had no right insisting she tell him.

"He's been having nightmares lately about his grandmother. That's all. I guess his imagination got the better of him. But that still doesn't excuse what he did, creeping into our room when we're asleep and stealing the key. What if we'd been making love or something? Imagine the horror on everyone's faces. No, that kid— and I'm betting Karl heard him get up and went to check—is off to his aunt's house for a week to teach him a lesson."

"C'mon, Becky, go easy on him. I mean, I often wonder myself why you're so adamant about keeping the room locked. It's not normal."

She hated it when he called her Becky. He only ever did so when he was trying to calm her down, believing she actually liked that.

"Because I don't want her memory dragged up ever again. That's why. And that's the end of it. If you don't like it—" She almost said go live with your own mother, but stopped herself just in time. That wasn't fair. Keith didn't know the real reasons, and if it was the other way around, she imagined she'd be pretty confused, too.

"If I don't like it, what?"

"Nothing, sorry. It slipped out. I just can't believe Ashley did that. He knew the consequences."

"You're really going to send him to your sister's?"

"I'm gonna think about it, yes."

Back when Rebecca's mother was getting more and more senile, it had been Rebecca's best friend's mother who had taken her under her wing. She letting Rebecca stay over on weekends, made sure she had clean clothes and did her homework properly. As the years passed, after her boyfriend was killed by a drunk driver, Rebecca's best friend, Caroline, had found religion. She became a devout, strict Christian, who believed in discipline and punishment. When Ashley was a toddler and they went to visit Caroline, she had started referring to Rebecca as her sister. It had stuck ever since. And Rebecca knew her children were scared to death of Caroline. For good reason, too.

"Well, maybe he did hear something—mice or a bird got in. I don't know. Perhaps we should go and have a look, just to put his mind at ease?"

"No! I've said it a million times, and I won't say it again. No one goes in that room. Not even me. The end. For God's sake; how many times do I have to spell it out?"

"Okay, okay, got it. But, maybe just threaten him or something about sending him to your sister's. For now, I'm sure he won't do it again."

"You're right he won't. I'll shove that key up my butt if I have to. Now, what plans you got for today? I thought we could go to the new shopping centre and check it out."

As if Keith thought he had any choice in the matter.

Chapter

6

Edna's Story

Rather than be shocked at the insinuations behind
Dorothy's actions following her ghostly appearance,
Richard acted the complete opposite. The first inklings
of suspicion and doubt had crept into Edna's mind
because of what the woman had conveyed to them—
supposing it wasn't a prank, after all. Now it didn't
appear to be the case—Dorothy had implied she hadn't
died the way Richard had said. He was nervous the rest
of the night, constantly heading over to the liquor
cupboard to top off his glass. When she asked him
about his thoughts, all he could talk about was what
had been confirmed—that the afterlife existed. Death
wasn't the end of everything. Maybe Heaven and Hell
really did exist. Or, even better, perhaps there was a
chance a person could return to the living world.

He'd started reading books on reincarnation,
looking for signs, for evidence as to why some
remained trapped in limbo as ghosts, unable to move

along, while others could return to Earth, albeit in the
body of another, he couldn't be sure. Surely, there had
to be a way, some trick or manner in which one could
choose to come back. And Richard became obsessed
with the subject.

They had another séance shortly afterwards,
Mary returning, as did the same friends as before. All
of them were eager to learn more, their hunger for
morbid truths a drug to them. As before, Edna refused
to take part in any of it, still finding it all repulsive and
twisted. Besides, she was now eight months pregnant;
they should be rejoicing in a new life, not an old,
deceased one. Richard had tried to insist on her sitting
with them, even raising his voice and insinuating
possible consequences if she refused. But, for once,
she stood up for herself. She reminded him that if
things happened as before and it was her that got
thrown from her chair while pregnant...

On that, he had to relent.

Again, Dorothy was summoned, yet they found
it impossible to get her to talk in any other way other
than through one knock for yes, two for no, which
made for some frustrating moments. When Richard
insisted to Mary that she try and explain why she
wasn't moving on, whether she could return in the
body of another, as before—Dorothy turned menacing
and violent, almost destroying the room in front of
their eyes before disappearing again. It was concluded

they had to try different methods of getting her to communicate.

But for now, that would have to wait.

Three weeks later, Rebecca was born, a healthy girl with sparkling green eyes—a gift from God. Even Richard forgot his obsession to proudly show his daughter to all his friends.

"She will grow up to have her father's charm, wits, and intelligence, and her mother's beauty," was his favourite saying. He'd said the same thing about Alison when she was born. Edna couldn't remember too many other times when he'd spoken of her at all. She knew he'd wanted a boy—not a girl. Someone to take over the business when he retired and well, a woman wasn't going to do that, was she? A business needed a man at the top; a women's place was at home. She had thought to remind him of all the things women had done during the war—important, *manly* things—but it would have made no difference. If she wanted to remain living under his roof, then challenging him was not going to help.

Now that Rebecca was born, it also meant Alison had someone to bond with. The poor girl who had few friends because her father didn't want the house run amok with kids and who also didn't want her staying over at friend's homes because she might 'get in trouble'. How exactly a five-year-old was supposed to get into trouble, she didn't know. His view was that so many kids in his house would lead to breakages, and well, she wasn't exactly going to pay to have them replaced, was she? So, until now, it had been up to Edna to keep Alison amused.

Now the three of them could go out on long walks in the park when it was warm and be joined by some of Alison's friends. Regardless of whether Richard was away on business or not, one of the maids would undoubtedly inform him if kids had been staying over or impromptu parties were set up.

Six months after Rebecca was born, Richard was back from overseas. And it seemed he had been doing more than just overseeing business. He'd been to some obscure country in the Far East, doing research, investigating. At least, this is what Edna gleaned from conversations he had on the phone with friends. And now he was ready to carry out another séance.

The party began to arrive shortly after ten. Edna made sure Alison was in bed and asleep, not leaving her side until then. One of the maids stayed upstairs with Rebecca, where she wouldn't hear anything and subsequently wake up. The maid was not to leave Rebecca's side unless it was highly important. The men barely acknowledged Edna as they entered the house—only their wives and Mary having the common courtesy to stop and say hello and ask about the children. As always, Edna told them the kids were fine, growing strong and that she was blessed to have them.

Everyone knew Richard's views on women, and his wasn't the only such opinion. The husbands of those in her house probably treated these women equally the same way. These women accepted it and probably told themselves every day that they should consider themselves lucky for having a husband to provide them with everything they could wish for. Edna should do the same, as they sometimes told her in private. But how could she when her husband was more interested in the dead rather than the living?

They all seated at the table, same positions as before with Richard at the head of the table, Mary by his side. But this time, there was an extra item with them. Richard had brought back from abroad a Ouija board, one that apparently had seen many years of good usage and had been blessed by some local vicar or witch doctor. Edna didn't know who or care. All she knew was that the stinging of her heart and acidic pulsations in her stomach made her extremely nervous.

"Welcome back, everyone," said Richard. "As you all know, I have been gone a long time, but not just on business. I decided to take advantage and carry out a little investigating of my own. You see, in other countries, those we might call primitive or backwards actually have a long and extensive history of dealing with ghosts and the afterlife. They don't see it as mumbo jumbo as many here in England do, but it is as accepted as waking up every morning and going to work. Perfectly normal, in other words. Reincarnation, in these countries, is a fact, not a superstition. The afterlife is accepted as this one we are currently living. I want to prove, once and for all, that it is true.

"We all saw what happened with the spirit of Dorothy, but communications were…difficult to say the least, so I acquired this artefact from a reputable source. With this board we can contact another spirit, anyone we so choose, and they can confirm to us that it is indeed possible to choose one's next destination before death."

A few excited murmurs of approval answered him in return. Mary said nothing, but Edna, from her usual position at the back of the room, thought she caught an element of unease in her eyes. She kept casting quick glances at the board as though it was something she should be afraid of. Something that might leap up and attack her at any moment.

"We are privileged folks, ladies and gentlemen. We've all been through some terrible times thanks to the Nazi's. Yet here we all are, if anything, better off than before the war. And I, for one, want it to stay this way. For a long, long time."

"But," interrupted one of the men, "if one could choose where to go once dead, why would there be ghosts? Why stay behind like that? It must be terribly uncomfortable, trapped in the body of a spirit. Why not just go to Heaven, or, as you say, choose to return in the body of another?"

"That's what we're going to find out, old chap. I want answers, so that when my time draws near, I don't have to give up everything that has taken me so long to build. I certainly can't count on my wife or two daughters to carry on my legacy, so I want to do it myself, one way or another."

This had been Richard's obsession all this time. He was scared to death of just that—death. The idea that he would grow old and weak and eventually die terrified him. That his vast wealth would be handed down to either his wife or daughters and probably wasted, his business enterprise ruined, was something with which he couldn't cope. And so this madman wanted to prove the existence of the afterlife, but not just that. He wanted to discover if there was a way to return reincarnated so he could carry on where he had left off. The idea was preposterous, but he refused to listen to reason. Even Mary had tried convincing him that it didn't work that way. But no, he insisted they exhaust every single possibility until a means was found, regardless of cost. She thought of the millions that had died during the war; were they given a choice as to where they wanted to go next? She didn't think so.

"Mary, would you like to begin proceedings?"

"Okay, everyone. Of course, we can't guarantee we will be able to contact the kind of spirit we are hoping for. Not are all willing. Not all are able to. But we must keep an open mind, and no one under any circumstances is to interrupt me if and when I do make contact. Now, I would like everyone to lightly touch the planchette with the index finger of their right hand, barely touch it. And again, do not interrupt me. Do not start asking your own questions. Same for you, Richard. Understood?"

They all nodded in approval. Edna wasn't sure if it was her nerves but already, as they placed fingers on the planchette, she sensed a change in the atmosphere. Like the build up to an electrical storm, the air charged with static, slightly more oppressive than before. She thought of her children sleeping peacefully upstairs and wondered why Richard couldn't just accept what he had rather than what he didn't. But she assumed it was the way of wealthy men, like spoiled children, always wanting the newest craze, the things they couldn't have.

"I think we should start with Dorothy. I believe she is still in considerable turmoil and we should try to help her move along to her next destination."

They all agreed although Richard didn't seem as happy as the others did.

"Dorothy, this is Mary again. Are you here with us?"

The tension in the air was thick, the silence and expectation something Edna could almost reach out and grab with both hands. A candle flickered, causing wicked shadows on the walls. Then, she heard the slightest of scratching sounds and a faint gasp from one of the women as the planchette twitched.

"Dorothy, is that you?" asked Mary

The planchette twitched again.

"Harold, you did that," said a woman.

"Quiet!" hissed Mary. "We want to speak with you, Dorothy. We're your friends, remember? Will you communicate with us?"

The planchette twitched along the board at first then moved slowly to the word '*yes*'.

"Good! Thank you, Dorothy. We want to know why you're still here with us. Why haven't you moved along yet?"

Edna inched closer to see what was being spelled out. She still wasn't convinced Dorothy was doing this rather than Mary, but curiosity had got the better of her. She watched as the planchette moved around the board before it then stopped.

Unfinished business.

"What business, Dorothy? Can we help?"

No.

Edna caught Richard glaring at Mary. He didn't care about Dorothy's unfinished business; he wanted answers to his own questions.

Evidently, she took the hint. "Tell me, Dorothy, once you resolve your issues and move on, where will you go?"

Another life. New life. Elsewhere. Beautiful life.

"You mean Heaven?"

Maybe. Maybe not.

"Can you choose where you'd like to go? To Heaven, or could you stay here longer in your spirit form? Maybe…return in the body of another?"

Richard was barely breathing now, his eyes bulging and unblinking, as he watched the planchette circle the board. Everything had come to this, what he was looking for.

Yes.

Gasps and little shrieks of disbelief or excitement broke the silence. Richard said nothing. He continued staring at the planchette with not a single emotion on his face. Edna thought she saw his hand shaking slightly, betraying what was surely occurring beneath his expressionless features.

"So, Dorothy, if you wish, you can choose to return to Earth in the body of another, as a newborn? Or move on to Heaven and live eternal joy and peace?"

Yes.

"Thank you, Dorothy. I hope you find what you're looking for. So ends this séance."

The moment Mary removed her finger from the planchette, loud exhales came from them all, chuckles, gasps of wonder, all panting heavily as if they'd been holding their breath. When Mary turned the lights back on again, there was the slightest hint of emotion on Richard's tanned face.

"Good God, Richard, we did it! It's true, then!" said one of his friends. "Heaven exists, and we can come back again and start over. It's truly amazing. I can't believe it. There's no possibility of it being a trick, is there, Mary?"

"We can only take her word for it, Henry. Many have tried to return, to prove there is life after death, but all have failed. I guess when our time comes, we shall all find out. But I have no reason to believe Dorothy would want to trick us."

Henry rose from the table, poured a shot of scotch, and handed it to Richard. Then he poured one for himself. "Congratulations, Richard, old boy! Your legacy will continue even after death! But how does one decide in which body to be reincarnated in? Maybe we should have asked her that? Can you imagine returning in the body of some poor family, almost destitute? That would be most horrendous!"

"I don't suppose it matters. From what I've read those that have been reincarnated know from a very early age that they have been reborn and who they were before death. I guess, in this case, it will be up to your wife, or more probably your daughters, to find you," said another.

Richard still hadn't said a word. He seemed to be under great shock following the revelation. Edna felt sick, these people talking about her as though she wasn't present. If it were true, maybe Richard deserved to be reborn to some homeless family. Maybe they all did.

Richard finally picked up his scotch and drank it in one gulp. The colour returned to his face.

"Rather quiet there, Richard. Sure you're okay?"

"Yes. Yes. I just need a little time to process what has just happened."

He rose and went and poured himself another shot. The others, including Mary, seemed to take the hint and rose themselves. The men all patted Richard on the back, speaking words of encouragement and felicitation while the maids brought their jackets. Soon, it was just Richard and Edna alone in the great room. He barely acknowledged her presence as he poured himself another shot. Edna headed upstairs to bed.

He wasn't sure if anyone had noticed, but Richard had been close to tears once that planchette spelled out the word 'yes'. Like a child, he had wanted to burst out crying, instead having to repress a sob and keep quiet so as not to betray the utter joy coursing through him. He had also been very close to screaming at them all that if anyone was doing this on purpose, a prank, he would kill them so they would get to find out for themselves if there was an afterlife or not. But he knew deep down it hadn't been a prank. Besides, they all knew how important this one was to him.

It was a common saying, usually among the poor and mainly said through envy, that money couldn't buy happiness. This was completely untrue, of course; money could buy a whole lot of happiness like the mansion he was sitting in right now, for example. The cellar was stocked with some of the finest wines in the world, a selection of cars he had parked out front. The list went on. And yet, at the same time, that saying was only partially true. Because what money couldn't buy him was time. Not the kind of time he was thinking of, anyway.

As soon as the war had ended and he realised the kind of rich pickings would soon be available, he jumped at the chance. Within a couple of years, he had more than doubled his already sizeable fortune. But with that came something else that seized him in crippling, fear-induced arms. He was now forty-four-years-old. One day he would die. His own father had done so from a heart attack at forty-seven. Richard didn't want to die. He was enjoying life too much—the power he held over others, his mistresses dotted around the country and world, the speed with which technology was evolving everything around him, cars becoming faster and faster. There were so many things he still had to do, but time was not slowing down for him; in fact, it seemed to be doing the complete opposite.

If his wife could give him a son, he might die safe in the knowledge that his business would continue to flourish long after he was gone, but that wouldn't happen with a daughter, would it? Women weren't meant to run businesses, be leaders. They were too weak. And then what happened? After getting pregnant again, this time—based on a law of averages, surely a much-coveted son—it was another girl. It was a sign. A sign from God—had to be. And so his terror and fear of death and losing everything had resurfaced like a recurring nightmare.

Now, though, those fears could be safely banished. His eventual death wouldn't be the end of everything, after all. All thanks to that stupid bitch, Dorothy, who had the decency to come back and tell them. Her death hadn't been completely pointless, after all.

Alone with his thoughts and a tumbler of scotch, he absently ran his fingers over the Ouija board. Such a good find. He'd stolen it from the old man, of course, after he refused to part with it. Now it was his. That old crone, Mary, wouldn't be needed much longer either, once he figured exactly how to summon other spirits. Then he could set about summoning the ones who would help him on his next journey—returning again in the body of another, once he died.

He picked up the planchette. Such a simple object yet its power vast. He fantasised for a while, running it across the board, having imaginary conversations with spirits, until he thought he caught movement out of the corner of his eye. It might have been the scotch, but he was pretty sure he saw a shadow dart out of view. When he turned in that direction, there was nothing to be seen. Could it have been Edna come to check on him? No, she would already be asleep with the girls. Ignoring it, he returned to his little game, a wicked grin on his face.

Hot air blew onto the back of his neck.

He spun around, knocking the tumbler to the floor that exploded upon impact.

"Who's there? Henry, that you playing stupid games?"

He looked around the room, searching for the intruder. If it was Henry or one of the others, they would pay sorely for scaring him like that. And for causing him to drop his favourite glass. When, after several seconds, no one revealed themselves, he assumed it must have been a freak draft come from somewhere. Darned house—the maintenance was a fortune.

Then he heard a soft scratching. When he turned around, he was both shocked and slightly bemused to see the planchette was moving across the board of its own accord. Bemused because it meant someone was trying to contact him. It meant he might not need Mary and could summon the spirits on his own from now on. Maybe Dorothy had decided to return again, the foolish woman. He watched as the planchette circled the board.

You caused this.

"Dorothy, is that you?"

Yes.

"What do you want? You were, umm, so very helpful earlier, thank you. Truly."

The bottles of scotch in his cabinet rattled.

It wasn't me.

"What wasn't you?"

It was a trick.

The bottles rattled harder, thumping against the glass door.

"Dorothy, are you causing that? Please stop and tell me what you are talking about."

The door cracked and flew open.

It wasn't me you spoke to earlier.

"No? Then who was it?"

Someone else.

One of the bottles fell from the cabinet and smashed on the floor, filling the room with the musky aroma of expensive scotch. Richard winced.

We lied. No afterlife. You die. Stay dead. In Hell.

You killed me. You pay.

Another bottle suddenly flew across the room straight for his head. He managed to duck just before it exploded against the wall. Another came, then another. The planchette was moving wildly around the board, writing seemingly random, nonsensical words. The chairs around the tables rocked violently as though invisible figures had grabbed each one in both hands and was banging it up and down on the floor. Like children throwing a tantrum. One of the paintings on the wall began to spin in circles, then fell, taking with it a large chunk of plaster. Another followed suit.

"Dorothy, stop! Why are you doing this?"

The planchette started writing slower again, while all around him furniture and ornaments rattled and shook as though an earthquake were taking place.

You killed me. No accident. You let me die.

"Dorothy, I swear I did not push you down the steps. You tripped. I rushed to get help, not to abandon you. You…you were very good to me. I miss you—our time together."

And then from somewhere, everywhere at once, came the most deafening, piercing scream he had ever heard—as though a dozen women were screaming in his ear all at once. He almost fell off his chair in his haste to back away, cover his ears, but it was as though the sound was coming from inside his skull. The rest of his scotch bottles exploded as if someone had just fired a gun at the cabinet. The air was filled with flying shrapnel, causing him to duck again, covering his head, diving under the table. Several vases shot across the room. Books fell from his bookcase, tearing upon impact, the pages fluttering up into the air like wings. Then, directly before him appeared two legs, covered in grime and blood that trickled down to form a small pool on the floor. The owner of the legs slowly began to squat, bending down to reach for him perhaps. Whoever it was, they were naked, their body covered in cuts and bruises and smelling foul. Like some of the homeless people he sometimes came across who hadn't washed in weeks.

Now, the whole body was visible except for the head. Two sagging breasts, a chest replete with infected-looking gashes and bruises, the semi-transparent skin a mottled grey like that of a decomposing thing. She wheezed, her face still hidden from him by the table. Too shocked to ask who it was, although subconsciously he thought he already knew, all he could do was stare at the impossible creature before him, waiting to see what it would do or say. The wheezing became a croak, someone's throat filled with phlegm.

Slowly, very slowly, the spirit-thing squatted further, revealing a filthy and bruised neck, two icy-blue lips covered in sores, a mere stub of a nose, and two eyes with nothing but the whites showing, her eyebrows furrowed into a frown. Her eyes were so large and bright he thought he could see his own reflection in them. Despite her deathly appearance, there could be no doubt it was his deceased maid.

"D-Dorothy, I…"

"*Die!*" she howled, and lunged for him, reaching out to grip his throat with both hands.

Richard screamed, jerked backwards, banged his head on the underside of the table. Instead of grabbing him, she passed straight through him and disappeared. He spun around in all directions looking for her, sweat soaking into his eyes, his heart in his throat. He circled several times before realising she wasn't there. Only when he was completely sure she was gone did he dare come out.

He surveyed the mess around him. How his wife and the maids hadn't heard all the ruckus, he didn't know. But he sure as hell wasn't going to clean it up himself. According to Dorothy, he had been tricked, but he didn't believe her. The afterlife existed—Dorothy herself was proof of it. No stupid ghost would scare him off from his ultimate goal—to join the likes of Dorothy in the next life and then return once more to start all over again. Forget Dorothy, anyway. She was just a disgruntled ghost. What harm could she do?

Richard headed off to bed, but first he left a note for the maids to clean up the room first thing before his wife and the kids came down. Then he found another bottle of scotch in the kitchen and took it with him to bed. He drank most of it before he finally fell asleep.

Chapter

7

Detective Tom Riddley parked outside Bradwell
Cemetery and lit a cigarette. He wasn't looking
forward to this meeting at all. Not that it was a
meeting, per se, but an investigation. He had an idea
his day would be completely ruined by the time he left
these grounds.

Why they had had to put this on him, he didn't
know. A local constable could just have easily looked
into it. It wasn't as if a murder investigation was going
to be started so what was the point in calling in a
detective? It was probably a bunch of kids. Halloween
was just around the corner and they probably decided
to make an early start. Although he had to admit, if he
did catch them, he would be hauling their butts off to
juvenile court with a recommendation that they receive
the toughest penalty. It was wrong, just plain wrong
what they had done. No one deserved that, especially
the families who would now have to go through the
heartbreak and sorrow all over again. If it wasn't kids,
then…yeah, okay, maybe a detective was best suited

for this particular case. Wouldn't be the first time weird cults had done similar stuff.

Tom stubbed out his cigarette, checked the rearview mirror and ran a hand through his mop of curly, brown hair. It sprang back up immediately. Forget it. The vicar wouldn't care too much about his appearance today. He could have used a shave as well, but the kids had been messing about in the bathroom, so this would have to do. Besides, he was used to dealing with drug dealers and pimps, so keeping up his appearance was hardly a priority in his day-to-day. And now this.

Reluctantly, he climbed out of the car and headed off to look for the vicar. If he remembered correctly, the local vicar was a small guy with a mop of cotton wool hair, frail and probably close to joining God. If the shock hadn't sent him on his way already.

The last time he had been inside a church was his youngest's blessing three years ago, and if it had been up to him, he wouldn't have bothered with that. Jane had insisted on it, or her parents would never forgive her. Tom couldn't care less either way. The doors to the church were closed, so he knocked, not quite sure of the protocol in such a situation, but as he did one of them eased open anyway.

He peered in and looked around. A man he assumed to be the vicar was at the back of the church near the altar. As the door creaked open and the vicar turned, he saw a glimmer of unease on the old man's face.

"Yes, may I help you?"

"Hi. I'm Detective Tom Riddley. I'm here about the, umm, incident in the graveyard."

The vicar's unease turned to relief as Tom headed down the aisle, brandishing his ID card. "Oh yes, thank God. Thank you for coming so quickly. I'm the vicar, as you can see. Dennis Nichols."

The man shook Tom's hand with a surprisingly firm grip for one so frail-looking. His back was hunched over slightly, and his face bore all the marks of someone who had led a long, maybe troubled life. His piercing blue eyes seemed too old for the rest of him. Maybe God had forgotten about him too at some point. That or the events of the early morning were deeply troubling him.

"I understand there has been a desecration?" said Tom

"Yes. I'll take you to it straight away. Terrible thing. How anyone could possibly do such a thing to a deceased person, I can never understand. Especially one who was as delightful and kind as Peggy Smith."

"You knew her?"

"Oh yes, she was a regular to the church. Passed away just a few days ago. Which makes it all the more horrific, of course. Her children will be devastated when they find out."

"So you haven't told them yet?"

The vicar wrung his hands together, then started picking at his fingernails. "No, I'm afraid not. First thing I did was phone the police, then I called Henry the gardener to block off the grave so onlookers couldn't see in. I didn't want to disturb the scene, either, because of…you know…evidence and things."

They arrived near the back of the cemetery where a high brick wall signified the end of the cemetery. A narrow road ran past. Large, wrought-iron gates were still locked, held in place by a thick steel chain. It was still only nine a.m.—too early to open the gates yet, surely.

"So just to confirm no one else knows except you, me, and your gardener?" asked Tom

"Correct."

"And how long ago did you stumble upon the desecration?"

"Umm, let's see. I woke around seven, made tea, then came for a walk around the grounds, as always. Henry comes along at eight, so I let him in. Then, shortly afterwards, he called me. That's when I phoned the police, about an hour ago."

Dennis took Tom to an area of the graveyard that had been cordoned off with rope tied around the trees. The ground was still fresh and damp from the previous night's rain. Tom really didn't want to look at the state of the corpse this early in the morning. The only time he had ever seen a badly mutilated corpse was when he'd worked as a constable, the occasional road traffic victim.

"It's a terrible sight, Detective. It will be haunting my dreams for quite some time."

Tom glanced at the old vicar. *I really didn't need to hear that, Reverend.*

With no choice but to inspect, he headed across the grass, weaving through tombstones, mindful not to step on anyone's grave. The phone call had come while he was still having breakfast, a quick bacon sandwich Jane had thrown together for him. Now it sat in his stomach like a lead weight, one that has been coated in poison.

A large pile of earth sat in front of him. He skirted it, one hand holding onto the taut rope circling the desecrated grave, and peered in. The large oak above him gave a lot of shade and made seeing the appearance of the corpse slightly harder. But he didn't need much sunlight to see the complete and utter desecration of the dead woman.

The lid to her coffin had been totally destroyed and removed from the desecrator's attempts at quickly getting to the body, probably with an axe and a crowbar. There were no houses in the immediate vicinity, so the only person who might have been woken by the commotion would have been the vicar. Tom guessed this man slept very well at nights thanks to his quiet surroundings. Even so, it was clear that a certain hastiness had been used to remove what was required from Mrs. Smith. The dress she was buried in had been ripped to pieces as well, opening up and revealing her chest. Her face was a mottled grey, lips blue, cheekbones and eyeballs already beginning to sink into her face where decomposition had begun. Her chest had been cut open, as if someone had performed a late and impromptu autopsy, the flesh jagged as though cut with a saw. A large hole sat there, evidently so the perpetrator could cut off and quickly and easily remove the desired items. Her ribcage protruded like some archaeological discovery, bugs already picking it clean. The organs were like dried pieces of fruit, sunken into her chest, shrivelled and useless. A large rat sat in her chest gnawing on one of them, maggots squirming all over her body, bugs appearing and disappearing from various orifices in her face. Tom wasn't exactly sure what he was supposed to do here, and he had little to no knowledge concerning the workings of a human body. But he was pretty sure it was just the heart that had been torn free.

The rat turned to look up at him, a small piece of flesh sticking out of its mouth, then bolted.

Tom had seen enough. He looked away in disgust, then back at Dennis, who looked on the verge of tears. He joined Dennis by the path.

"Terrible thing, isn't it, Detective?"

"Yes, it is. I'm not much of an expert, but from what I can see, it's her heart that has been taken. And they were very quick and efficient about doing so. I don't suppose there would have been any witnesses?"

He shook his head. "No, I'm afraid not. The nearest person who lives around here is me. I assume they climbed over the gate, retrieved the poor woman's heart, and left."

"Well, I'll call the forensic team to check for fingerprints, but I don't suppose they'll find anything. Any idea why someone would steal her heart? Whoever did it was probably aware she had only just been buried, so I don't think it's a coincidence."

"Well, it wouldn't be the first time it has happened."

"What? *Really*?"

"Oh, no, unfortunately. Several years ago, we had a spate of desecrations occur. Let me see…about ten years ago, three or four bodies were desecrated. Police never caught them."

Tom racked his brains. Could there be some satanic cult operating in Bradwell somewhere? As far as he was concerned, if there was, it was probably just a bunch of kids listening to heavy metal, smoking, and dressing in black all the time. Stealing dead people's organs took it up a notch, though.

"Well, unfortunately there's not a lot I can do right now. Once forensics are finished your gardener can fill in the grave again, or whatever needs to be done. But unless we catch them in the act or someone hears something, I don't have a lot to go on."

"I understand, Detective. I really hope this doesn't start up again like the last time. It's terrible for the victims' families."

Tom thanked him for his time and left. The last thing he had expected when he arrived was having to think about Satanists. Just what the hell did they expect to achieve with a dead woman's heart apart from time at the hospital with some virus?

When he reached his car, he phoned forensics and gave them the directions. He had somehow managed to keep his bacon sandwich down, but thoughts of Mrs. Smith having been torn apart meant it floated somewhere between his throat and stomach.

"Please don't let this be the start of something," he muttered to himself, and lit a cigarette. Because if it did, he thought he might consider a career change— shelf filler at the local supermarket, perhaps.

Chapter

8

As soon as the kids left for school, Rebecca sighed in relief. The habitual chaos and noise in the house so early was going to kill her today. That or give her a record-breaking migraine. Either would be just as bad. She slumped into a chair at the breakfast table, nursing a coffee, and swallowed a couple of paracetamols. Hair tied back in a ponytail to avoid it drifting into her eyes, she took another sip of coffee hoping and praying it stayed down. She guessed she probably should have stuck to fresh orange juice, but that wasn't going to wake her up, so coffee it was.

As soon as she woke up, she felt the familiar bouts of nausea running through her stomach, first trying to recall what she'd eaten the night before, then when she did, partly wished she hadn't. Might have been the Chinese Keith brought back last night as well. She'd always had her suspicions about exactly what ingredients were used in it. Considering she tried to keep herself to a pretty strict diet since the kids were born to avoid getting fat, she wondered if she really should start to consider getting more of a grip on things. The kids' laundry wouldn't get washed or their beds made if she laid around in bed all day with a dodgy stomach, feeling sorry for herself. Not after making questionable decisions like she had last night.

Besides, she really didn't feel like it, but this morning was the anniversary of her mother's death, three weeks ago, and she had to go leave flowers. She would happily sell her soul to not have to go this morning, but there were certain things out of her control, and she had no choice. The old bitch still controlled her life even in death. More so in death, even.

The paracetamols finally kicked in, which was helping to ease her stomach. The cemetery gates would open in about fifteen minutes, so hopefully she could get in and out without being too distracted by anyone. Especially the local vicar, Reverend Nichols. He looked harmless enough, but under that candyfloss hair and those dinosaur eyes, he was a man who knew far more about certain things than he liked to give himself credit for. He was old and wily like a fox, always with an eye on what happened in his village, taking in all the gossip the parishioners liked to feed him and forgetting none of it. When her mother was buried, the Reverend's face had been a combination of loathing and relief; she saw it in his eyes. Relief that she was dead and loathing that she was being buried in his graveyard, as though she might rise up one night and come for him. It was like burying the Devil in his own back yard.

Rebecca pushed herself to her feet, forcing herself to go get dressed so that her mind wouldn't keep coming up with excuses to avoid going to the cemetery. She tried to focus on good things but struggled to come up with anything. Not even her kids, who had betrayed her trust in them the other night. That would take a lot to forget, and not just the terror at hearing they'd been trying to break in the room.

She threw on some clothes, didn't bother with any makeup as she rarely did, and left before she lost her resolve. It was only a ten-minute walk from her home, so she grabbed some flowers from the local florist—nothing too expensive—and was soon at the graveyard. The front gates were already open, which meant Reverend Nichols would be up especially early this morning. Why, Rebecca had no idea. The gates were *never* open this early. Did the locals usually have a date with death so early in the morning? Queuing up at the gates as they did at the supermarket? It was downright morbid.

Today, though, it seemed she was the first and only visitor so far.

She hurried along the winding path, old and decaying gravestones to her left and right, now covered in moss and bird dropppings. Squirrels darted back and forth among the graves, dashing up the large oak trees dotted around the grounds. On another occasion, it might have been quite peaceful to come and sit in here, perhaps read a book or contemplate more philosophical matters. Some of the graves in here were over a hundred years old, the headstones as decayed as the skeletons beneath them. But not today. Today she just wanted to get in and out as quick as possible and head back home.

There had to be hundreds of graves in here as well, which signified a serious lack of space already so her mother's grave was right near the back. As Rebecca headed down the path that took her there, she saw Reverend Nichols talking to someone on the opposite side. The man wore a grey suit, and they stood near an area that looked to have been cordoned off. Then she saw the mound of earth and guessed who the handsome-looking stranger was—a detective, surely, come to investigate a disturbance. From here the man looked barely thirty. She decided to eavesdrop.

The Reverend had his back to her, so he didn't see her wandering aimlessly around, reading the inscriptions on the various graves. But the detective did. He cast a few glances her way but didn't appear too concerned with her overhearing their conversation. And they were apparently discussing a desecration. From what she could gather, there were no witnesses, but a recently deceased elderly lady's coffin had been smashed open and her heart removed.

A shiver sauntered up Rebeca's spine, her whole body tingly as though the proverbial goose had walked over her own grave, but she had no plans to die yet. The detective didn't sound as though he had much of a clue about what to do about it, either. The vicar was obviously distraught, and for good reason. She vividly remembered the last time something like this had happened in his cemetery. She had been both terrified and horrified and also recalled the first time it happened, some twenty years ago. The village had been shocked and dismayed by such a terrible, cruel act of violence. It seemed one couldn't even rest in peace nowadays.

The vicar and the detective finished their conversation without any clear plan, it seemed, so she quickly headed back towards the direction of her mother's grave. She found the headstone—the cheapest available, a simple rectangular slab sunk into the ground—and knelt beside it. The flowers she'd brought last time were as dead and wilted as her mother, drooping over the side of the rusty metallic vase as though hanging their heads in shame. She took them out and threw them to one side. Even the grass around the grave had turned brown and dead, a stark contrast to the lush green everywhere else in the cemetery. It was like a permanent stain on the grounds, where everything in the immediate vicinity perished, as if marked by her mother's rotten soul, contagious and corrupt. Even the weeds struggled to push through the soft soil, barely making it a few inches above ground before wilting. In life, her mother had been tainted by death, and now that death had joined her in body and spirit, its unbiased grip now spread out around her like a polluted shoreline. It made Rebecca feel even more sick than she already was.

Feeling like she was about to vomit, Rebecca replaced the old flowers with new ones and said a short prayer, more for herself than her mother.

"I hope they accept you, Mother. Take you in. It was never your fault, more Dad's, but you let grief blind you. What you did can never be forgiven. Not by me, it can't, anyway. Hopefully, God will take pity on you. Hopefully, He won't allow your little schemes and plans to come to fruition, because if He does, I swear I'll stop you myself—at whatever cost."

She had said it with determination and belief, but even she knew deep down her prayer would fall on deaf ears. The signs were already there, and Edna had only been dead for three weeks. She thought about the desecration that had occurred across the graveyard and briefly considered doing the same here. If it had been up to her, she would have cremated her mother then spread the remains far and wide. Down the drain, perhaps, or far out to sea. But Edna had insisted in her will that she be buried, and Rebecca was pretty sure she knew why. The bitch had planned everything right up until the end.

She rose, her legs now prickled with pins and needles, her head slightly dizzy, feeling like she'd been here far too long. She didn't want to think about how things might be the next time she came—perhaps armed with a spade and a crucifix, not to mention a large bottle of holy water. Maybe she should have planned ahead herself and brought some holy water with her today. Her son's incident suggested it might not have been a bad idea.

Rebecca was about to leave and go home, when she happened to glance back at the flowers she'd placed moments ago—Pink chrysanthemums, a handful of them that had been among the cheapest at the florist and whose bright colours she found stunning. Her garden was filled with them. But now, she could only watch in horror and disbelief as the colour faded from them, as if some dark shadow had passed overhead, obscuring their brightness. Like watching a nature documentary set at high speed, the pinkness faded completely to grey. The flowers wilted, resembling the dead ones she'd thrown away. The petals fell one by one, now a dirty black, and were blown away by a sudden breeze that had picked up, leaving a skeletal stem behind. The vase was knocked over, perhaps by the wind, and a rust-coloured water ran out, seeping into the dead grass. The remains of the flowers blew away too, perhaps trying to escape the foulness surrounding this entire area and what lay beneath.

Disgusted, Rebecca kicked the vase away, then spat on her mother's grave. "Go to Hell, Mother. I hope you rot in Hell."

Without another word, she left.

Chapter

9

My dearest Vera,

You've always been my best friend, the one always there for me, so I feel I can only confide in you right now.

I don't know what has happened, but it is something surely terrible and malignant that has taken Richard's mind. He is barely coherent anymore, at least as far as his thoughts are concerned. He stays up into the long hours of the night in the study where they did those horrible seances. The doors are locked, and he refuses to let me or anyone else in. I can't remember the last time he even spoke to his daughters. Alison is understandably beside herself with grief and confusion. She thinks she is responsible somehow, something she has said or done. No matter what I tell her, she won't accept her father's ways right now.

I tell you this, Vera, because I too am scared and don't know what is to become of all this. The man frightens me with his words and suggestions, ideas so alien to me it beggars belief. I can't remember the last time I saw him eat. Not anything substantial, anyway— just the occasional sandwich the terrified maids prepare for him. They have noticed a change in him as well and are trembling messes around him, scared he might shout at them or worse. But, of course, they don't know the real reasons behind his sudden madness—his ideas.

Since the last séance, his friends and the medium have not returned, but I know he has been conducting them on his own. I hear him in his study at night, when I come down for a glass of water or juice. I hear him chanting out questions one after the other, and I hear that terrible scratching the planchette makes as it circles the board. I also hear other voices in there with him. At first, I thought he had a maid in there with him. I'm not so blind and naïve as to know where my husband's eyes fall sometimes, his dark desires. After the events of the séance with Dorothy, I have my suspicions as to what went on between them.

But you see, Vera, that is the least of my worries right now. I know I fail to please him as much as I once did, before I was pregnant, because I'm so tired all the time now. I am just someone to raise his children (for all he cares about that) and keep up appearances. Can't have the rich tycoon divorced and his ex-wife taking his precious wealth, can we? Of course not!

The last few times I heard him in his study with that Ouija board, I decided to snoop, see what he was doing and the kind of questions he was asking. For it was clear to me that he believed himself to have made considerable progress, as though he didn't even need Mary the medium anymore. I listened in, aware that he wasn't calling for Dorothy anymore, but anyone who happened to be in the vicinity. And he had found someone.

At first, he asked questions and received replies via the planchette. Then he asked the spirit to show themselves. Even from outside the room, with its thick walls and heavy oak door, I could feel the drop in temperature. I heard things rattling in there, bottles perhaps, the clinking of glasses, the faintest sound of the window rattling against the frame.

Who are you? he asked.

I heard what sounded like whispers, which almost made me scream. It was hideous, a woman's voice, but something about it was wrong. Like this person didn't have a proper grasp of the English language or had some kind of speech impediment. The woman answered him, but I didn't catch what she said

Why are you here? he asked her next. Why haven't you moved on?

Again, I didn't catch everything she said in that horrid, creepy voice of hers, but I did catch the last part. Like it here, she said.

You don't want to go to Heaven? Are you not allowed to go?

I like it here. Want to stay here.

And then, I am positive I heard her say she wanted to return again, start all over anew. This is what Richard had been wanting to hear all this time. I could practically feel his eyeballs bulging, hear his heart thudding in his chest. I imagined him sitting bolt upright in his chair, waiting to hear more from this spirit, demanding answers.

Except, in barely a whisper, he said, And can you? Can you return?

Yes, she replied.

Show me how. Tell me. I want to know now.

She then proceeded to speak to him very quickly, to the point I couldn't understand a word she was saying. Richard said nothing, either; he was listening intently to her. Again, I imagined his eyes bulging from their sockets, a big drunken grin on his face like he gets sometimes. But then, the spirit's voice stopped suddenly, as though cut off.

Come back, yelled Richard, making me jump. Wait. Then he swore at the empty room, filthy, horrible words. I heard him get up, his chair fell over, and then he was mumbling to himself.

Quickly, I left in case he caught me. That would have been disastrous, given his foul mood. And yet, when he came to bed and I half opened an eye, that big, silly grin of his was plastered all over his face. I feared he had been given the news he so desperately sought.

Of course, I was right. But what was to come of it, Vera, fills me with terror for the future—both for myself and especially that of my beloved daughters. It's why I'm writing you this letter now, so you have it in written form as evidence should anything happen to us. Please, if you do not hear from me in a month's time or you phone and they say I'm not home, go to the police, take this letter and tell them what I'm about to tell you.

The next day, after overhearing Richard's conversation with the spirit, he was quiet, subdued, which made me nervous. I felt scared to be around him. The maids obviously felt the same because whenever he came into the room, they were jittery, unable to look him in the eyes. And yet, what made me even more nervous was that he was acting different around me, being polite, smiling. He even kissed me on the cheek, and I cannot recall the last time he did anything like that. He asked me about the children, their schooling, if they were happy, healthy. It may have been the first time since either were born that he showed—or pretended to, at least—any interest in them or their wellbeing. And it scared me, for I knew he was up to something. Richard is not affectionate around people unless it's for a reason, like when he wants something from them.

That evening, after dinner, he was unusually talkative and nice, even managing to make me and the girls laugh a few times. It was just like when I first met him. He sent the girls off to play with one of the maids and told me he wanted to speak to me. It was a life-changing event, he told me. I guess with hindsight I should have seen it coming, but a part of me still believed this was all just a rich man's game. A wealthy man with too much money who doesn't know what to do with himself anymore. That, combined with the fact he obviously wasn't getting any younger, that he was starting to worry about old age and losing everything. He said that very thing during one of the seances, remember. But anyway, he sat me down in that same study, poured me a glass of sherry, and told me to listen very carefully.

We're not getting any younger, Edna, he said. And the world is becoming a dangerous place. There's talk of the Russians maybe starting another war. You saw the damage the atom bomb did; the Russians have the same weapons now. And really, anything could happen. Imagine the girls being caught up in a nuclear war, everything destroyed. It would be like a new Ice Age. Is that what you really want for your girls?

But that's between Russia and America, Richard. We're safe in England. And besides, I'm only thirty-three, hardly an old lady. But what are you saying, you want to move elsewhere?

In a way, yes. But no one is safe from nuclear war, Edna. I—we—could lose everything. We'd be desolate, nowhere to go, dying from radiation poisoning. I wouldn't wish that on anyone, let alone the poor girls. We could start fresh elsewhere. We could, umm, hide, until it all blows over, come back and start again. Completely new.

But what about the house? You're going to take that with us? I asked him.

My spine froze when he replied to my question. I should have known what this was all about.

Where we would be going, we wouldn't need it.

What do you mean, we wouldn't need it? You'd buy another house, in another country? Somewhere safe from the threat of war? Because we saw what happened in the last war, Richard. And much less from those bombs they have now.

No, I wouldn't be buying another house. The world we inhabit would be our house. You've witnessed the seances. You've seen that there is proof of the afterlife. Well, since then, I've been conducting my own seances in private. I have been shown a way where death does not have to be the end of everything. That we can continue on long after our deaths, again and again. We can be reborn.

What are you talking about, Richard? You're scaring me. Those seances were nothing but pranks. That Mary was tricking you, trying to get to your money, no doubt.

Of course, I was lost for words. Even so, I still didn't expect what came next. The man is mad, Vera, utterly mad to think this might happen as he plans.

Not pranks, Edna, but very real. I've seen it with my own eyes, here in this very study. I want us to end our lives, Edna—you, me, and the girls. We will end our lives, live in purgatory for a while until the world is safe again, and then we will return. In the bodies of others, we can start again. We could even stay on these grounds; we don't have to actually go anywhere. We can haunt these grounds until it's safe, then return. Be reborn in the body of a baby, not have to worry about growing old, and our memories will remain, so we will know to find each other again. I have trusted friends who will take care of my business so that when I am old enough, I can take back what is already mine. We could, in theory, live forever. But I can't do it on my own. I need you with me. What do you say?

He was asking me to commit suicide with him, Vera. Kill the girls, as well, and supposedly we would all haunt our home for a while before returning again, reincarnated. Can you believe that? Madness. It's sick. How could he possibly expect me to kill my beautiful girls, and then for us all to hang around until the world was safe again? I told him, no, absolutely not, and that it was madness to even consider such things. Alison is four, Rebecca is still a baby. We would go to hell, not return as ghosts.

When I refused, he became furious. Said it was my duty as his wife to obey everything he said and did. I told him murder was not included in my duties when we made our vows, to which he had no response. Instead, he threw his glass at the wall and stormed from the room. We haven't discussed the matter again.

So you understand my terror now, Vera. I fear he will go ahead with his plans, regardless of what I said, and I don't know what to do. Take the girls and run, or hide and lock ourselves in their room at night? God help us, Vera. I am terrified my husband will kill us all.

That's it. Now you know, so please, guard this letter somewhere safe. Although I fear it may not matter. I will phone you in a few days' time, if only to let you know we're still alive.

Take care, Vera. Please pray for us.

Chapter

10

Two days later and Ashley still lived in fear, expecting at any moment for his mother to grab him and say '*right, you're off to Aunt Caroline's for a month*', but it still hadn't happened. Maybe she was tormenting him on purpose, making him suffer, drawing out the mental torture, letting him think he'd got away with it. Then, when he least expected it, *bam*! Off they went to his Aunt's. Sometimes, he wished she'd just get it over with, tell him and Karl they were off and let the punishment begin.

Every time he came home from school, he tentatively walked in, terrified to see his mother standing there with her arms folded across her chest, as she always did when annoyed. Maybe she'd have a rucksack beside her with a few clothes thrown in. No games or the PlayStation, of course, because that would be part of the punishment. But again, it didn't happen.

His father hadn't said a word to him either, no friendly pat on the shoulder or even a wink. He didn't offer any words of comfort, either: *Don't worry, son, your mother will get over it. Just keep out of her way for a while.*

It made Ashley wonder if they were conspiring against him. Even Karl had been avoiding him these last two days, as though by doing so, his part in the events might be forgotten. And yet, with his mother quieter than usual, lost in her thoughts, he guessed he could finally banish the threat of Aunt Caroline from his mind.

When he sat down to supper that night, he ate without a knot in his stomach for the first time in what felt like years. Even Karl seemed to be back to his usual self, joking with dad, their mother smiling at their jokes, albeit weakly. When it was his bedtime, he hugged his mother, hoping the gesture might be the final element to wash away any lingering doubts she might have about sending him off, and went to bed. What he had learned from all this, was that he was not going to try and enter that room ever again, no matter what he heard and saw.

He hadn't heard anything since then, either, leading him to wonder if he'd imagined it, after all. Not a sound from that room, not a single mention of Grandma since. It was as if she'd never existed. So, he lay snugly in bed, all thoughts of Grandma also banished, and within minutes he was fast asleep.

At first, still groggy he assumed it was Karl messing with him again. Now that things were back to normal, so was Karl, up to his mischievous self. When Karl tugged on his foot for the third time, Ashley's annoyance turned to anger and he lashed out blindly, not caring if he kicked his brother in the face.

"Go away, Karl. Leave me alone."

He pulled his feet back up under the covers, curled into a fetal position, and tried to get back to sleep. Starting to doze off again, he yelped when someone grabbed his foot more forcefully, dragging him a few inches down the bed. That hurt. Now fully awake, his anger full blown, he hit out again, almost knocking the covers off the bed.

"Piss off, Karl! Go back to bed or I'm gonna tell Mum tomorrow. She'll send you to Aunt Caroline's for sure."

Ashley brought the blanket up again, waiting for Karl to leave. It was pitch black in his bedroom and he couldn't see a thing. But he could hear him, breathing heavily as he tried to stifle a giggle. It was late by now, so why the sudden urge from Karl to ruin his life? Ashley couldn't hear the TV on downstairs, either, so his parents must have gone to bed as well. Which meant it had to be well past midnight. This caused a sliver of unease to ripple through him. Why would Karl be up at three in the morning, messing about?

Before he could answer, Karl grabbed his foot again, but this time, instead of letting go, he dragged him halfway out of the bed. And for the first time, he realised the hand gripping his ankle was icy cold, so much so that it hurt.

"Hey! Stop! Who is that?"

He flapped around looking for the lamp switch, but by now he was nearly falling out of the bed, trying to grip the sides to avoid ending up on the floor.

"Karl, is that you?"

But how could it be? Ashley was nearly double the weight of his brother. There was no way he could drag him from bed like this. Panicking, he tried to scream for his parents, for his dad to come and save him from whatever this was, but the breath was taken from his lungs. He could only manage wheezed gasps as he flapped about on the bed trying to find something to maintain his grip.

He landed with a thud on the floor. With his other leg, he hit out at whoever was dragging him across the room, but missed them completely. He was vaguely aware of a dark form before him—large, much larger than Karl—but now he knew for sure that there was no way this could be his brother. For a brief instance, he wondered if it was his father, finally come to collect him and take him to Aunt Caroline's. But he knew this wasn't true, either. The form that had him half in and half out of his room was too big, too fat to be his dad.

"Help!" he wheezed, but he might as well have whispered for someone to come for him.

He grabbed onto the doorframe with both hands, frantically trying to wriggle himself free with his legs, but was merely kicking at thin air. When his hands were snatched away, he tried punching the floor with his fists in the hope of waking his parents or Karl, but the thick carpet muffled all sounds. Whoever was dragging him along the floor was also wheezing, a great bulky outline that he now thought he recognised, and that made his panic grow.

Then, what he somehow knew would happen, did. The door to his grandma's room swung open, creaking ominously. Ashley sobbed, pleading to be let go, but his vocal cords felt paralysed, his heart wedged in his throat. He scratched feebly at the soft carpet as he was pulled along, now halfway inside his dead grandmother's room. She was going to lock him in there forever and would do all kinds of depraved things to him. He would die in there, horribly and slowly.

The moon was peering in through his Grandma's window so now he could see more clearly the thing dragging him in as he desperately fought to hang onto the doorframe again. It felt like he was going to be pulled apart, split in two at the waist, his intestines thrown everywhere. The person had their back to Ashley but he recognised that huge bulk, the thinning grey hair on the top of her head like wisps of smoke, the elephantine thighs beneath the flowery dress that might once have been a curtain. It had been real, after all. He wasn't dreaming or hallucinating. She was going to lock him in there with her forever.

His grip loosened on the frame, the final tug-of-war over his body being won by the thing that might have been his dead grandmother.

"Help!" he called again with the last remaining ounce of strength he possessed.

Chuckles came from inside his grandma's room. His vision started to blur from the desperation, the room swimming before him. His fingertips gradually slipped from the frame until they flopped onto the floor. Ashley closed his eyes and waited to be dragged completely in and for the door to slam shut forever.

But then something else happened. He felt a prodding on his head, gentle tapping. Was this a trick to get him to open his eyes?

"Ashley, wake up," came a soothing voice.

"No, leave me alone. It's a trick, I know it is. Just do whatever you want to do."

"Ashley, you're dreaming. C'mon, get up. Get back to bed."

He shook his head, knowing it wasn't really his mother standing over him, but her, his dead grandmother. She wanted him to see her face before she did whatever cruel things she had planned for him. "Go away,"

Then he felt himself being lifted and dragged from the room, and only then did he dare open his eyes. "Mum? Is that you?"

"Yes, Ashley. Get in bed. Go to sleep."

"But…but it was Grandma. She dragged me out of bed and took me in her room. She was going to lock me in there forever."

"You were having a nightmare, Ashley. And sleepwalking. Your grandmother is dead. Now c'mon, stop messing about."

He allowed himself to be led to his room and tucked in again. His mother bent over and kissed his forehead.

"So how was the door open then, if I was imagining it?"

"I don't know. I guess I forgot to lock it. Now go to sleep."

Then she left him and closed his door behind her. He heard a key locking the other room and then the only sounds of his thudding heart and his quiet sobbing. If he wasn't going to get sent to Aunt Caroline's after this, he never would. He just prayed she didn't lock him in the basement for too long.

Chapter

11

It was Saturday, which meant no school, and that was just fine with Ashley. He was tired and terrified at the same time, once more expecting his mother to pack him a rucksack and ship him off to Aunt Caroline's. But when he trudged sheepishly down the stairs to breakfast, she wasn't anywhere to be seen. Only his dad sat at the breakfast table, sipping coffee, eating toast, and reading the newspaper. Karl wasn't there, either, which was strange; usually he was up long before Ashley.

"Hey, Ash," said his dad as he entered the kitchen. "Sleep well?"

What to say? Tell the truth or say nothing and wait for the punishment? Maybe his dad even knew. Surely, mum would have told him? Ashley shrugged and grabbed a bowl and his cereal. "Where's Mum and Karl?"

"Your mother had to go out for a while, and Karl has gone with a friend to the park. Just you and me. Everything okay? You look tired."

It was now or never, then. Ashley had always known his father never liked Grandma and was as glad as anyone when she died. Perhaps he could give him some answers. Because Mum had been lying last night when she said he'd been sleepwalking. He'd seen the fear in her eyes himself. "Remember the other night when I thought I heard noises in Grandma's room and wanted to check it out?"

His Dad's eyes lit up. He obviously hadn't been expecting this. "Yes, and that was stupid, by the way. Your mother wanted to send you both off to your aunt's. You were lucky I talked her out of it. Why do you ask?"

"Last night I…something happened. Mum said I was dreaming and sleepwalking, but I know I wasn't. Look." He lifted his pyjama bottom and showed him his ankle. It looked as though someone had tied a length of rope or something around it, an ugly red ligature mark that ran all the way down around his ankle.

"Jesus, Ash, what the hell is that? That looks painful. Has your mother seen it?"

He shook his head. "No, but…last night, someone grabbed me by the ankle and dragged me out of bed. It was pitch black, and I thought it was Karl messing about, but it couldn't have been him. There's no way he could have dragged me out of bed onto the floor. I was kicking and lashing out but hitting nothing. I would have kicked him.

"Then, I got dragged across the floor. The door to Grandma's room was open and she—I'm pretty sure it looked like her, at least—tried to pull me in. But just before she did, Mum came out and stopped it. She said I'd imagined it, sleepwalking, but I didn't imagine this, did I?" he said, pointing at his ankle.

"Jesus," he said again. He was holding a piece of toast mid-air, halfway towards his mouth and had suddenly turned pallid. He couldn't seem to take his eyes off the bruise around Ashley's ankle. "You say someone *dragged* you into that room? The door was locked. Only your Mother has the key. How'd it open?"

"I don't know. It opened by itself. Mum said she must have left it open by accident."

"Bull. Not after last time. I always wondered if this might happen. Or something like it. We should have had her cremated, but even so, it's just not possible. Can't be."

"What exactly happened, Dad? I know you were both relieved when she died, and I overheard you talking once about things she had done. But…but she's dead. Isn't she? How can this be happening? Is it, like, her ghost or something?"

He said nothing for a moment, evidently considering his words. Ashley thought he might throw up at any second, such was the tension running through his body. That sentence, 'I always wondered if this might happen', suggested they had been half expecting this. Whatever 'this' was.

"No, it's not her ghost. Not like that, anyway. Your grandmother, you see, had a very tough time when she was younger. When your mother was about your age now, she went through a lot. Then things happened, and she got confused. Misled might be a better word for it. She got involved with some things she should have stayed well clear of. But we never thought anything would come of it. We thought it was just her being grief-stricken, and losing her mind a bit. We were even going to have her admitted to Northgate Hospital for the Mentally Impaired, but she refused. And when she lost that bloody mansion and had nowhere else to go, we had no choice but to let her move in with us. God awful woman! Should never have agreed to it..."

"But...I still don't understand. Is she, like, dead, or not? Did she not die at all but just pretended or something, and Mum has her locked in there? 'Cause I've heard noises coming from in there loads of times, and it's so weird Mum won't let anyone go in there. 'Cause ghosts, if they're real, can't grab people around the ankle and drag them off, can they?"

"Your grandmother was thrown out of church years ago. Things she did. And said. There was a big scandal. She was dabbling in...stuff. Stuff she shouldn't have done. But we didn't believe it! Like I said, we just thought she went a bit mad, so we tried to ignore her. Yes, of course she's dead! What happened last night, what you think happened, it's impossible. I saw her dead body myself, saw her carried out of here.

"So yeah, I'm inclined to agree with your mother, Ash. It cannot have happened as you said. Maybe you were dreaming and banged your ankle when you fell out of bed."

"Dad! You just said you believed me! I didn't fall out of bed. Nor was I dreaming. Something dragged me from bed. Why don't you believe me all of a sudden?"

"Because it can't be real, Ashley. It just can't. Your grandmother did and said some stupid stuff, but not that. I refuse to believe that. Not in this day and age. Christ, a couple of hundred years ago they'd arrest us for blasphemy and burn us at the stake."

Ashley was shocked. Seconds before his dad had been telling him that Grandma had been doing bad stuff, and that it might indeed have been her last night, even though she was dead. Now he was saying the complete opposite. He wanted to cry over the injustice of it all. If it had happened to Karl, they would have taken him to the hospital and burnt that room down, called a priest in or whatever they did in such cases.

Right now, he didn't even want to be in this house anymore. He'd rather take his chances at Aunt Caroline's house, Bible-basher or not. The idea that tonight he would go to bed and that there was a chance—a very good one—that the same thing would happen again, filled him with a terror like he had never known. If they refused to believe him, he was going to sleep on the sofa downstairs or with Karl. He could tell all his friends at school if he liked; Ashley didn't care. Anything was better than sleeping alone in his room again.

Aware that his father wasn't going to give him the benefit of the doubt, he threw his spoon in the cereal bowl and stormed off upstairs to his room to get dressed. He wanted out of this house right now, even if it meant spending all day in the park alone.

Keith finished his toast and coffee although his appetite had been ripped out from him. Now a heavy weight sitting in the pit of his stomach. This moment had been building for weeks, years even, both him and Rebecca dreading the time when Edna's threats may become actions. He had never really believed it himself, assuming—as he had just told Ashley—they were empty threats from someone who should have been committed years ago. So the other night when Ash had said he heard noises coming from in that room and had then tried to go inside, he nearly had a heart attack.

They both agreed that Ashley must have imagined the noises, typical from kids, perhaps watching too many horror movies on the internet, but now this. There was no way Ashley had done that to his ankle by falling out of bed. That was a handprint there, the marks of the fingers clearly visible. He wasn't going to tell him that, though. It was strange that Rebecca hadn't said anything to him this morning before leaving in such a hurry. So something was going to have to be done, but what? That stupid, old bitch had been getting involved in stuff she had no right to, making threats to his family all because of what happened before.

But the way things were looking just lately, those threats may not have been as empty as they seemed. There was only one thing for it. Hopefully, Ashley, who was in a bad mood because he didn't believe his story, would get dressed and leave for the morning. At least until lunch time. If and when he did, Keith would take action, a little responsibility himself, because Rebecca sure as hell didn't appear to want to get involved.

Keith tried to focus on reading the newspaper but found it nearly impossible. All he could think about was what the old bitch may have done before she died, what she had set in motion. She had to be stopped. He'd dig up her grave if necessary, burn her body then scatter her ashes everywhere. Or he would do to her what some sick individual had done at the cemetery yesterday. Fortunately, Keith was right. He soon heard stomping coming from upstairs, then a door slammed shut slightly more forceful than necessary, and Ashley came thundering down the stairs.

"I'm going to Paul's," he yelled, and left without waiting for a reply.

Good.

Keith threw his newspaper down and headed upstairs. Hopefully, he'd have all morning to himself to resolve this issue once and for all. It was silly, childish, and negligent of Rebecca to pretend nothing was happening. She knew more than anyone the possible dangers. Instead of facing them, she preferred to lock the door and pretend her mother had never existed. Well, not anymore.

He knew she kept the key to the room under her pillow so Ashley couldn't go sneaking around again, but she hadn't thought about him investigating his mother-in-law. Keith picked it up, his heart in his throat as though stealing something from his wife, and headed back outside to the landing.

Now that he was there, he wasn't really sure if he could go through with it. There could be anything in there. Maybe Ash was right; Edna's body had been replaced with someone else's and her rotting corpse was in there instead. Maybe Rebecca had gone senile like Edna and wanted to keep her remains here forever. Or maybe she was still alive, somehow resurrected. Or maybe she hadn't died at all, everything a big plan for her to continue her mad scheme.

He took a deep breath and inserted the key. Or at least tried, because his hand was shaking so much.

"C'mon, Keith, get a grip," he muttered. "There's nothing in there. It's just your wife being paranoid."

Makes two of us then, doesn't it?

He finally managed to insert the key and turned the lock. The click as it turned sounded like a gunshot in the quiet of the house. Another deep breath and he opened the door.

The first thing to hit him was the musty, mouldy smell of an unaired room. Like stepping down into the basement for the first time in years, the particles in the air made him sneeze. It was dark, too, the curtains having been closed the moment the room was locked and never opened again.

"Hello?" he muttered, then regretted it, feeling like a fool, or some idiot in a bad horror film. As if anyone would answer him.

He threw open the door and stepped in, flicking the light switch. But, just like everything else surrounding the old bitch, the light was dead. Everything was exactly as it had been when Edna died. Even the bed was unmade, as though Rebecca couldn't wait to close the door and memories on her mother. But the room seemed empty. No old crone was hiding in a corner, stumbling about the place, or hiding in the shadows, waiting for him. An old television sat in the corner, the box type that still had dials to change the channels and a dresser with a filthy mirror smeared with something Keith did not want to even think about. A large wardrobe was the only other piece of furniture in here that Keith had never even opened. There was even a bucket beside her bed should an emergency occur. Keith had no intentions of looking to see if there was anything inside it.

When Keith parted the curtains slightly to see better, he regretted it. Dotted around the corners of the ceiling were old spiderwebs, their original creators having either died or moved elsewhere to look for fresh pickings. In some of them, flies were still bound and gagged. More flies lay dead on the windowsill, seemingly contradicting the spiders' thoughts on lack of supplies. More lay on the floor. Where so many had come from, he didn't know, especially since the window had been closed for the last three weeks. But the important thing was that Edna was not here, waiting for him with her flabby, outstretched arms, ready to drain the life from him. Ashley had been mistaken, after all, it seemed. Not surprising really; Keith had had a few nightmares about the woman as well.

He turned to leave the room, still thinking about that ligature mark on his son's ankle and how he might have gotten it when there was an ominous creak in the room. In the silence, it sounded like a distant scream. Before he could even turn around to see what had caused it, he felt the hot, foul breath on the back of his neck, rancid like the smell of rotting vegetables. A hand gripped the back of his neck, icy and freezing that immediately reminded him of the marks on Ashley's ankle, and he was dragged backwards toward the wardrobe.

A cackle sounded, like an old crow, long fingernails digging into the soft skin on his neck causing a warmth to trickle down his chest. He swung wildly with his arms, trying to connect with whatever was dragging him back, but all he connected with was thin air or the wardrobe's open doors. Thoughts of a prank played through his mind as he wheezed and gasped for air; maybe Ashley had sneaked back into the house and this was his way of paying him back for not believing him. But he knew this wasn't true. He knew it as much as who that arm belonged to, that grim stench blowing onto the back of his neck, the huge weight dragging him into the wardrobe.

He writhed and struggled, frantically looking for something to grab onto, to prevent himself from being pulled further into that dark prison where he may never see the light of day again. He tried to recall the words both he and Rebecca had memorised shortly after learning of Edna's wicked plans—the words that would keep her at bay—yet his mind was on lockdown, quarantined in another realm not so different from the one Edna occupied.

The thing behind him snarled like a threatened dog. He felt warm spit on his flesh as it cackled and chuckled. And then he tripped as his feet collided with the frame of the wardrobe and he fell halfway in, still with one hand gripping him by the nape of the neck. He used both hands to hold onto the sides of the wardrobe, screaming for someone to come and rescue him. His wish to be left alone in the house for the morning was now his deepest regret. His fingers slipped on the woodwork, and he was helpless as he was finally dragged inside the wardrobe. The doors slammed shut, trapping him in darkness with the woman that should be buried several feet below ground in Bradwell Cemetery. His screams were then abruptly cut off.

When he opened his eyes again, his initial thought was that he was dead and that Edna had killed the rest of his family. Rebecca was standing over him like a sentinel, glaring down at him, and he was vaguely aware of the two boys laughing in the background. A sense of abject dejection washed over him, the idea that Edna's plans had finally come to fruition. But when he looked around and saw that he was in bed, his thoughts on having died and gone to Heaven seemed unlikely.

"You're awake," said Rebecca in a cold voice.

Keith tried to sit up, but a sudden stabbing sensation in his back caused him to groan and fall back again. He muttered an expletive and tried to check himself for all possible injuries, but there was only an icy feeling on the nape of his neck, as if he'd been lying on a pack of ice cubes.

"She got me," he groaned. "Edna, she was in her room and she got me. We have to stop her now, before she gets the kids."

"Keith, you were—"

"No, no, listen. I went in her room because of Ash's ankle and she was there. She grabbed me around the neck and dragged me into the wardrobe. I'm telling you, Rebecca, we have to stop her now before it's too la—"

"Keith!" she said more forcefully. "I came home a little while ago. You were asleep in bed. You had a nightmare, just like Ashley, for God's sake. From Ash, I might expect it, but you're a grown man. Act like it. I'm fed up with all this crap about my mother. She's dead for God's sake! Now let it be."

She stormed out of the room leaving Keith bewildered and shocked. Yet, more than that, he was angry and resentful, because he knew full well his wife was lying. He could always tell when she was. She wouldn't look him in the eye, and she spoke to him in that condescending voice of hers, as though talking to the kids. He realised in that moment that if this was to stop, it would be up to him and him alone.

Chapter

12

Edna's Story

A week passed and, so far, Edna's fears about something happening to her and her children were ungrounded. She kept a close eye on both Alison and Rebecca, and she trailed Richard around the house when he was alone like a shadow, always keeping to the corners, just out of sight. He would sit in his study, reading books with titles and images on them that the girls must never see. He was obsessed with the Ouija board, locking himself in his study. Edna, pressed against the door listening in, would squirm and grimace at the horrible noises and sometimes jumping back in horror to then see shadows that flitted back and forth inside from under the door.

The chilling, haunting whispers reminded Edna of the injured and dying soldiers back when she worked at the hospital during the war. The simple fact of knowing Richard was in there alone, having conversations with entities and spirits caused goose bumps to riddle her body. It was sick and twisted; the dead should be left alone, not bothered or asked questions about resurrections and rebirth. And the reasons behind his incessant questioning and demands for answers were what made her see him as a repugnant individual who only cared about himself and his morbid desires for eternal life.

She often considered bursting into the room, demanding the spirits leave. She dreamed of grabbing that board and the planchette with its eerie scratching and throwing them into the fire. Then she would be cursed with Richard and put a stop to this nonsense once and for all. But if she did any of that, she would only achieve what she had been seeking to avoid in the first place—the death of her and her beloved girls. For Richard, just lately since she had refused his request, had become even more bad-tempered, snapping at her and the girls over the slightest things. He refused to eat with her anymore; instead, eating alone in that hellish study of his with his ghosts. The maids visibly squirmed every time he called for them. On many occasions, when Edna had gone to eavesdrop, he had demanded of them more than what they were paid for, their grunts and groans an indication of what Richard wanted. Two had already left without giving any warning, and Edna was sure she overheard them discussing the possibility they might be pregnant.

Yesterday her friend, Vera, phoned her after having received her letter. Edna had burst into tears, terrified for her life but especially those of her daughters. Vera tried to convince her to go to the police, but Richard was a very wealthy, very well-known man. His influences meant that he would have been informed by an officer at some point and once again, the consequences would have been unthinkable. Richard's wrath held no boundaries anymore. All she could do, she told Vera, was keep a close eye on the girls and pray that Richard found another way to satisfy his insidious demands.

Richard was in a foul mood, slamming doors, snapping at the maids over the slightest of things. From what Edna could gather from the phone call he just made, a deal for some lucrative business partnership had just fallen through, meaning he would lose thousands. He hadn't left the house since his discussion with Edna, and she hated this, wishing he would just go away for another six months and leave them in peace.

Another maid, tired of his constant shouting and ranting, had left just this morning, meaning they were short-staffed. Edna would have to help out with the laundry herself, while the remaining two maids attended to other chores.

She should have guessed, in hindsight, that Richard would insist and the possible consequences of denying him, but last night, Richard had come to her again, begging her to reconsider his proposal. Demanding that she follow him in leaving this life and starting again in another time, but she had refused. She called him sick, insane, and insisted he leave her in peace. The look he gave her, as he left, was of bitter hate and resentment—the kind he gave clients when they rejected his services. It said, *You will regret this*.

With Rebecca crawling around on the floor beside her, Edna folded the laundry. Alison had been left in the toy room next door with explicit instructions not to leave. The poor girl was now terrified of her father and his bad temper, and there was no way she would have gone with him without advising her mother first. Life in the mansion had become a nightmare, despite Edna regularly buying her all the latest dolls and games available to keep her amused and out of Richard's way. And Alison had also taken to her new sister as expected, virtually inseparable. So, that Richard was in his study and Alison happily playing with her dolls next door should not have given Edna any cause for concern.

Until she heard the scream that came from downstairs, abruptly cut off as though the person had had a hand clamped over their mouth. Or worse. At first, she thought it had been one of the maids, another so-called accident, just like Dorothy. So her rush to find out what had happened wasn't as desperate as it might have been otherwise. She picked up Rebecca and ran outside, calling her maids names. It was when both of them appeared from an adjacent room that Edna's heart felt as though it was being squeezed tightly. And when she burst into Alison's toy room and saw she wasn't there, her heart became a ball of ice.

"Alison? Where are you?" she yelled.

When her daughter failed to respond, Edna did panic. She almost dropped Rebecca in her desperation to find Alison. She ran downstairs, screaming her daughter's name, and almost bumped into Richard as he came from up the basement stairs.

"Where is she? Where's my baby?" she screamed at him. When he failed to answer her, only stared at her with absent, bloodshot eyes, she grabbed him with her free arm and shook him, demanding to know what he'd done.

"She...she fell," he muttered. "She's down there. You need to call an ambulance, quick. What was she doing down there, anyway?"

For a few seconds, his words didn't connect in her mind, as though he'd suddenly taken to speaking a foreign language. Dorothy had fallen down there; surely, he was referring to her. But then she heard what sounded like muffled groaning and dashed down the stairs, Rebecca now crying in her arms as well.

Edna screamed when she saw the outline in the poorly lit basement at the bottom of the stairs. Almost tripping herself and doing Richard's job for him, she made it to the bottom, put Rebecca down as gently as possible given the circumstances, and hesitated to cradle Alison. The girl was groaning very softly, her leg and arm bent back in a manner that human limbs were never meant to, a pool of blood growing under her. There was a hideous lump on the side of her neck where it may have snapped.

"Oh no. Oh, my baby, what happened? Call an ambulance!" she screamed at the tall, dark shape at the top of the stairs.

She wanted to hold her daughter, cradle her, but her body was so broken she didn't know where to touch her for fear of breaking her even more. Alison was like a ragdoll lying there, left to wither away and rot.

Alison tried to say something, but blood seeped from between her lips and all she could do was gargle feebly.

"Did he push you, honey? Tell me. Did he do this?"

Whatever Alison said in response was unintelligible.

Edna turned again to once more scream at Richard to phone the ambulance, but he was gone, presumably doing just that. There was no way Alison had come down here alone; she was scared of being attacked by giant spiders or bugs or ghosts even. Here, the exact same spot where Dorothy had also met her end. Then Edna recalled that nasty little gleam in Richard's eyes last night.

When she turned back to Alison, the girl's eyes were now glassy and Alison was dead.

The ambulance came and took her away some time later. Then the police asked what had happened, and Richard—Edna being in too much shock to speak—told them what he told Edna, that Alison had come down here by herself, must have tripped and fallen to her death. The police offered their condolences and no investigation was suggested. Edna spent the rest of the day cuddled up in bed with Rebecca, refusing to see or speak to anyone.

And she would have spent the rest of her life cuddled up to her remaining daughter, but now she had added responsibilities—making sure the same thing didn't happen to Rebecca. It had been Richard who threw Alison down the stairs—nothing would convince her otherwise. The evidence was too strong, the coincidences too obvious. She wanted to kill him herself. Had she been strong enough of both body and mind, she might well have attempted to, but her grief was too prolonged and overwhelming.

He tried to talk to her about it, tell her how sorry he was and that he would spare no expense in ensuring Alison had the biggest gravestone in the local cemetery, the most expensive coffin, but this all fell on deaf ears. Who cared how expensive the coffin was? Alison certainly didn't, and no amount of money would bring the girl back again. As far as Edna was concerned, they could bury her daughter in the back garden. She guessed Richard had killed her, to prove a point or as payback, and the damage was done. Never in all her life had she felt such hatred for a person. Not even Hitler and the Nazis who had ruined and destroyed so much of the world, caused so much death. Richard was worse than that; he had purposefully killed one of his own, his daughter. Out of spite. She was sure of it.

In the days that followed, she refused to speak to him or even be in the same room as him. At the funeral, that rage had overshadowed her own grief, hearing him pretend to sob and shed crocodile tears, telling all the family and friends that flocked to the funeral how grief-stricken he was for his poor, baby girl. Even Mary the medium and the original group that had come to the séance were there, and as before, they ignored Edna and her crying baby. Only Mary offered a few words. Maybe she knew the truth, too.

Richard didn't mention his idea to her anymore, either; instead, preferring to lock himself in his study and speak to his new spirit friends. Occasionally, Edna liked to listen in on him once Rebeca was asleep. Her body shivered with cold hatred and disgust when she heard him asking a spirit one night if it could see Alison. If the girl's tiny, little spirit was floating up in the ether with all the others. It made Edna sick, as though Richard was using the girl as part of his experiment, just a test subject for his warped ideas. All he cared about was where the girl's soul had gone to rest. And his obsession only grew worse.

Just two weeks after Alison's death, he
organised another séance. Edna heard him on the
phone, barely speaking above a whisper, as if he might
be ashamed or had a guilty complex. But Richard felt
guilty about nothing. She was surprised he'd waited so
long before bringing his morbid friends back again.
But this time, despite the grief and hatred clinging to
her like a second skin Edna decided she wanted in on it
this time. Now she had her own motives for wanting to
hear from the other side.

As the guests began to arrive and took their
seats, Edna said nothing of her intentions. She told the
maid to stay with Rebecca, sleep with her in the same
bed, if necessary, until she returned. Then she took up
her usual spot in the corner of the room, waiting until
everyone was seated. Mary was the last to arrive.

Richard listened to further condolences from
his friends, accepting them graciously. Seeing that
made Edna's stomach lurch. She wanted to tell them
all what had *really* happened, to see what they said
then. Instead, she kept quiet, biting back the sob at the
back of her throat.

"Thank you all for coming again. As you know,
we have been through a terrible time, but it is for that
very reason I brought you all back again," said
Richard. "Since the last time we were reunited, I
haven't been idle. In fact, I've been busier than ever.
We have proven that life after death exists, and much
more than that. I have subsequently discovered that

reincarnation is another proven fact, having spoken to many spirits in the last few weeks. Tonight, I intend to contact those spirits so that they may give us the key to returning in another life once we too are gone."

The Ouija board and planchette were set upon the table like ancient artifacts, jealously guarded. This time Richard didn't ask Mary to do the honours but laid his finger on the planchette first. The others followed suit. That was when Edna decided it was time. She grabbed a chair and headed over to the table, sitting at the opposite end to Richard without saying a word.

All eyes turned to face her, then to Richard, their eyes wide, jaws dropped, as if a ghost had come to sit with them rather than his wife.

"I want to reach out to my daughter," she said matter-of-factly. "I have a right to be involved. She was my daughter, and I want to contact her."

She caught a flicker of unease on Richard's face, a quiver of a smile that failed to develop any further than a twitch. He coughed nervously, looking around at all the others who waited impatiently for an answer to this intrusion. Not a single one of them said a word to Edna.

"Edna," said Richard, gently but with an undertone of impatience she knew well, "I don't think it would be wise for you to sit with u—"

"Alison was my daughter, and I want to contact her. I have a right to do so. This is my home as well."

"It's not about whose home it is or who has rights. These are my guests, and you have not been invited. May I suggest you go see to our other daughter. Another time, perhaps, you can join us."

"No, I will not. All this time you've been contacting spirits while I stand over there in the corner and not once have any of you so much as said hello or offered any condolences. Do you want to know how I think Alison really died? Shall I offer my thoughts, darling husband?"

It was like watching a tennis match as the heads of the guests followed the conversation, left, right, left, right. None of them responded to Edna's accusation, but none of them dared to look her in the eyes.

"Edna," he said a little more forcefully, "I won't repeat myself. You're making an embarrassment of yourself. I suggest you leave now please before you say anything you might regret later."

"Is that a threat, Richard?" Her heart thudded in her chest, the outright hypocrisy and patronising in front of his friends too much. She could feel the heat rising to her cheeks as though the blood boiled inside her, slowly climbing to her head. "How dare you say I'm embarrassing myself when all I want to do is communicate with my dead daughter? Why aren't you trying to contact her, Richard, with your fancy board and tricks? Not once have you even asked me if I'd like to. You've spent every night since she died communicating with your spirit friends, yet not once did you bother with your own deceased daughter! Now, why is that?"

Richard's face turned a bright shade of red. He rose from his chair, forced a smile at his friends, and headed in Edna's direction.

Before she could suffer the indignation of being dragged from her seat, she rose. "It's okay. I'm going. I know you don't care in the slightest about your dead daughter or your living one, but let it be known I shall be contacting Alison myself. I shall find my own answers to many things, and I will be happy to share them with everyone. Good night and have fun with your morbid, sick games."

Edna rushed from the room and headed straight to her bedroom, where Rebecca was fast asleep. The maid sat in a chair beside her bed, reading to the girl. Edna told the maid to leave and crawled into bed with her daughter, kissing her gently on the forehead. If Richard thought this was the end of the matter, he was wrong. Very wrong.

Chapter

13

With each night that passed, Ashley found it harder to get to sleep. he was too scared of someone coming for him. He had seen in movies where they would put a chair under the doorhandle so the door wouldn't open. When he tried it, the chair simply fell over. Then, he considered his desk, but this was heavy and should he need to go to the toilet in the middle of the night, the dragging of it would wake everyone. He'd even thought of trying to stay awake until his parents went to bed then sneaking downstairs and sleeping on the sofa, but that never worked out either. He was asleep long before his parents were despite his terror.

His anger at his parents was another reason he usually found sleep so hard to achieve. His mother didn't want to even listen to his complaints and his dad; he had sat there and told him bad things about Grandma and then suddenly turned the complete opposite direction and basically accused him of lying. Not even the mark around his ankle, which was still there two days later, had convinced either of them. It was still cold to the touch even now, his finger almost glued to it when he touched it.

He'd thought of asking his brother if he had heard anything, to see if this was all directed solely at him, but he felt a little stupid asking his kid brother such an important question. Karl looked up to him almost as his hero. What would he think if he told him he was scared of a dead grandmother? Karl would scare himself to death just talking about it, anyway. So that was out of the question. His only option, he figured, was that at the slightest indication of a ghostly visitation or if anything grabbed his ankle he would scream again as loud as he possible could. To hell with his parents getting annoyed at him. That sounded a lot better than being dragged into that room again. Safer. As an afterthought, he remembered the other night when he had been incapable of screaming through sheer terror, so he left a large glass beside his bed on the floor. If necessary, he could quickly grab it and throw it at the wall. That would surely wake his parents.

Ashley lay back in bad that night, trying not to think of grandmas or cold fingers wrapping around his ankle, and so, of course, this was all he could think about. That, and not understanding his parents' attitude to what was occurring, dismissing it completely. Neither of them had even offered to go in there and check to make sure it was empty. It wouldn't have taken more than ten seconds to ease his suffering, but his mother refused to even do that. Dad said he didn't know where the key was, which Ashley considered a lie. It was while thinking about asking a friend to come stay over this weekend—perhaps he would be able to hear things too—that Ashley's eyelids grew heavy and he fell asleep.

It was a pleasant dream, even though it involved his late grandmother. She was younger, much younger, almost his mother's age, and she was smiling, a full mop of dark hair that reached almost down to her waist and a slim figure, not the hanging blobs of flesh from her arms and flabby thighs he knew from her last years. He was lying in bed and she was telling him what a wonderful little boy he was, the first-born that made him so special. Then she gently ran a finger across his cheek, which made him giggle and cringe. She did it again, running her long fingernail down his cheek and then nicking his lips. It stung like being injected with a hypodermic needle. It caused his eyelids to flutter and he absently ran a hand across his mouth, which made it sting even more.

He opened his eyes.

He was annoyed at waking up more than anything because that was how he wanted to remember his grandmother. The previous version that would embarrass him in front of his brother and friends, by insisting on hugs and having to kiss her cheek. Yet, at the same time, despite that she was nice to him, always telling him what a handsome young man he was. She told him stories about when she lived in the huge mansion and all the deer and animals that would creep onto the grounds at night. But all that was now forgotten; his lips hurt.

He leaned over to turn on the lamp when something caught his eye in the far corner. His curtains weren't entirely closed so a sliver of moonlight poked through the window and there was a shape in the corner that shouldn't be there. It was as if his mother had moved his wardrobe, a dark shape tall and wide. He rubbed the sleep from his eyes, his stinging lip now forgotten about and squinted to see what it was. And then he saw more clearly the outline. It wasn't his wardrobe, not unless his dad had reshaped it into the figure or an obese person.

Now he was wide awake again. He leaned over once more to fiddle with the lamp switch when the shadow moved, turning slightly to face him. Two silver spots like distant stars flickered at him. He immediately opened his mouth to scream, but as before, something was blocking his vocal cords—maybe his heart, thudding high up in his throat. The shape shifted again, taking a step closer to him. He could hear its breathing, wheezy and rasping like a strong breeze blowing through a slightly open window. Two arms raised, as if beckoning him for a hug. Hunks of flesh dangled below the triceps, wobbling like jelly. And then he knew. Especially seeing those sparkling eyes that shone like silver coins, he knew. It was her, come for him once again.

All rational thoughts abandoned him. The glass sat on the floor beside his bed forgotten. His only focus was on that immense bulk staggering towards him, ready to drag him off again into whatever realm she occupied.

"It's okay, Ashley. Don't be scared," she croaked. "It's just me, your grandma, come to see her little baby grandson."

Ashley pulled himself into a tight knot, knees tucked under his chin, trying to back away from the advancing figure. She looked exactly the way she did when he caught a peek of her the day she died, except now her skin was leathery and grey, dark veins snaking across her face, the flesh sagging as though ready to drop off.

"Go away," he mumbled. "You're not real."

"But I am, Ashley, baby. I am so real. More real and alive than ever. And it's all thanks to you, the first-born…like my little Alison, so important to making a grandmother feel alive. And that's what you do. You make me feel alive. You will do, anyway, when the time comes. Now, why don't you give your grandma a hug, like the old times?"

She was standing over him now, as large as life, and yet he could see the far wall through her, a semi-transparent figure giving away her true self. Ashley tried to conjure a scream again, but he could barely breathe, let alone draw in enough oxygen to make it happen. It was as though his grandmother had sucked all the air out of the room. He could smell her, though; that horrible smell of old flowers that followed her everywhere when she'd been alive, now tinged with the stench of wet soil and rot. Fat fingers reached down and skimmed his cheeks, burning them.

He flinched, his bladder almost betraying him, the only part of him that seemed alive. "Go away," he squeaked. "You're not real. Mum!" But what came out was barely above a whisper.

"Grandma loves a first-born, Ashley. She just wants to show you how much. How you make her feel alive. Give Grandma a kissy, little Ashley."

She bent over then, her great sagging breasts dangling in his face, swinging from side to side as though trying to hypnotise him. The stench of fresh dirt, rotting flowers, mould was even stronger now, like in the basement sometimes when he went down there.

"I have such a big surprise coming for you. You're going to love it. Soon, Ashley. Your mother can't stop me now. No one can. Don't you love surprises, Ashley? You'll be able to live with Grandma forever and ever. Now doesn't that sound like fun?"

"Mum!" he squealed again, this time slightly louder. This gave him confidence. He inhaled another lungful of air, prepared to scream himself hoarse, when she bent over and kissed him, her lips cold as ice. They felt jagged and raw, as though he'd just been kissed by a dead, rotting fish.

The scream he had been building up to now came out in a splutter, covering himself in snot and saliva. Her breath was rancid and foul, causing bile to shoot up to his throat. And then he did scream as she rose again, a wicked, malicious grin on her putrefying face. She slowly bent over, perhaps to kiss him once more, when Ashley heard a sound—something he had been praying for the last ten minutes—that of a door opening. Unable to move any other part of his body, his eyes turned to the open door of his room, hoping against hope it was his father or mother. Instead, it was Karl, frowning and rubbing his eyes as he headed towards the toilet, stumbling along as though drunk.

When Ashley was about to scream for help again, he realised that his grandmother had vanished. The scream for help bubbling away behind Ashley's lips also vanished.

He spent the rest of the night staring absently at the far wall, wondering if it was possible to die of fright.

Chapter

14

Detective Riddley listened incredulously as the dispatcher told him to return to Bradwell Cemetery. There had been another desecration in the early hours and Reverend Nichols was extremely distraught. The dispatcher also said he may have some valuable information this time, possibly a witness even. No one had touched the desecrated coffin yet, and forensics would be there shortly, so he was to go have a look at the damage and wait.

He'd only been awake a couple of hours and this was not how he had envisaged his day playing out. Since the previous desecration, he had no leads whatsoever. No kids had been seen running from the scene. No satanic cult had been hiding in the shadows, claiming to have done it. And forensics had found no fingerprints on the deceased's body. It might as well have been a ghoul that did it, risen from its grave for a late-night snack and then returned to its underground dwelling place. Tom had hoped it would blow over.

Just kids, probably drunk, who thought it might be funny to scare the local priest. But now, if there was another, the chances of that were unlikely given the local media attention right now.

Could this be the beginnings of a serial graverobber? And what if it got worse and developed from stealing a dead person's organs to…doing worse things to the bodies? There were several necrophiles currently residing at Northgate Hospital for the Criminally Insane, so it wasn't as if it was the stuff only of horror novels and films. Tom really did not want to deal with necrophiles at this stage of his life and career, so he quickly headed over to visit Reverend Nichols, praying he had a witness or something.

He arrived at the cemetery and, as before, found the place to be deserted. At least of any living folks. He knocked on the church's doors, a resounding boom that caused pigeons to scatter and the odd squirrel to scurry off to safety. It was like knocking on the doors to Hell, so loud was it in the silence around him. Tom waited for a while, was about to knock again when he heard the clicking of shoes on tiles. The door swung open and Reverend Nichols stood there, looking as if he'd aged twenty years since the last time Tom saw him.

"Reverend, I came as soon as I could. I was told there's been another."

"Correct, Detective. This is most terrible. Shocking. What is wrong with people these days?"

"I have no idea, Reverend. Seems to be getting worse than better. I was told you have some information this time. Perhaps you could explain while you show me the desecrated grave."

"Of course. Follow me."

The vicar led Tom to the back of the cemetery near where the previous grave had been dug up. There was no sign any more of that desecration—the hole filled in and the grass skilfully put back to how it was before.

"So, as I told you before, I came to do my rounds this morning at around eight when I thought I saw movement from a distance. At first, in my groggy state, I thought it was one of the smaller trees moving in the wind or a branch or something. But trees don't suddenly run off and climb up and over fences.

"Concerned, I headed over to where the person had been lurking, and then I saw the mound of soil. I confess, in that moment, I forgot all about the intruder and was more concerned about what they had been doing in my cemetery. Here we are."

The vicar led Tom near the back of the wall where the mound of soil was and a large hole in the ground.

Whoever had done this must have been extremely fit. Tom couldn't imagine how long it must have taken to dig a hole that big and deep. It wasn't exactly scorching at night, but it was still warm enough that the person would have been drenched in sweat by the time they finished. This alone made him think it had to be a team effort. Again, as he got closer, he felt like he was approaching some unspeakable horror that had been buried deep beneath ground for a reason. Or as if something might suddenly reach up and grab him, drag him down into Hell. It was a creepy, ominous feeling, knowing he was about to see something that might cause him more nightmares for the next few nights.

Tom took a deep breath, glanced at Reverend Nichols, who looked rather pallid himself, and dared to peer over the mound and into the abyss below. There were no overhanging trees this time, so the view was crystal clear.

"Jesus Christ," he exclaimed, then immediately regretted it, given his location and company. "Sorry," he muttered.

"No offence. I may have uttered something similar myself."

Tom looked away then dared to look back, knowing he had no choice in the matter. When he joined the force to become a detective, he knew the day would come when he would be confronted by unspeakable horrors. Another woman lay there, he guessed middle-aged, and again recently deceased. Fortunately, he didn't have to worry about bugs and worms crawling all over her. What he did have to worry about was being greeted by the open cavity that was now her chest, reminding him of seeing gutted cows and pigs hung up at the butcher. The person, or persons, who had done this had evidently been in a hurry and may have used an axe to open her up rather than a saw. There were deep gashes all over her body, including her face where the perpetrators had been hacking away and had, on occasions, missed the target. Her head had been almost split in two, like a watermelon dropped on the floor, revealing all the messy insides including part of her dead brain.

One of her large breasts had been completely hacked off and lay beside her in the coffin. The other was also split straight down the middle, the flesh inside now grey and bloodless. The thieves had eventually managed to open her chest up though, and it looked as if it had been pried apart by their hands to reveal all the organs inside. As before, Tom wasn't too sure what each organ or intestine was, but he knew where the heart was supposed to be and what it looked like. As with the other victim, it too was missing. The remaining organs were now withering and lifeless, like dried pieces of fruit. Even her arms were nearly sliced off.

Tom turned back to Reverend Nichols who wore the same look of horror and disgust as when Tom had arrived. He couldn't blame him; he probably looked just as bad, especially with that morning's breakfast rising dangerously towards his throat.

"I'm no detective, of course, but it looks to me as though the person was in something of a hurry. I cannot begin to understand what the motives might be for doing this to the poor woman. Again, she was a parishioner of mine. I knew her well. Her husband will be devastated."

The words 'satanic cult' began to creep into Tom's mind with more determination. In Northgate there were a couple of offenders who had worked under the guise of cult leader, but it had always been assumed that was just an excuse to hold orgies with underaged girls and boys. Nothing ever suggested their get-togethers achieved anything in the slightest. They had admitted to sacrificing cats and dogs and drinking each other's blood, though. But right now, all that was irrelevant because unless evidence of some kind was found later on the victim or coffin identifying the perpetrator the chances of catching them seemed extremely slim. Then he recalled the vicar's words about seeing someone run off.

"So, you said you saw a person running away from the scene this morning. Did you happen to get a good luck at them? I'm guessing from the state of the deceased's body, it had to have been at least two men to dig up the coffin. It was warm last night; that's a lot of work."

"Unfortunately, no I didn't get a very good look, I'm afraid. I was in too much shock and surprise at seeing someone here so early in the first place. I do remember the person was wearing a dark jacket and had dark hair. Blue jeans. I didn't get a look at their face, so I don't think I could identify them."

"And it was definitely just one man? You didn't see another."

"Oh no. It wasn't a man; it was a woman. Of that I'm certain."

Chapter

15

His wife was lying. Ashley had been right, after all. Just as she had told their son he had been dreaming, that what he experienced was a vivid nightmare—which Ashley vehemently denied—so did Keith know full well he hadn't been dreaming the other day. He could still feel that wretched breath on the back of his neck, the icy hand that had gripped him around the throat, the smell Edna had taken with her to the grave, tarnished with the smell of decomposition.

Exactly what reasons Rebecca might have for deliberately lying to him he couldn't fathom. It was obvious she was hiding something, but exactly what that was, Keith couldn't guess. Something must have happened when Edna was alive, or perhaps long before then, before Keith had even met her, that she was keeping secret. Something she was forbidden to discuss or was perhaps too scared to share. He knew about Rebecca's sister, of course, and her father. Not all the details, but enough to know that Edna had gone quite senile at some point in her life and had never fully recovered. He knew she had been dabbling where she shouldn't and the repercussions may have been quite serious. It was along these lines that Keith considered there to be a connection.

Rebecca's father, Richard, had been obsessed with the afterlife, she told him, and had gone to extreme lengths to prove its existence. That had involved Edna, but Rebecca had always been rather coy when it came to explaining what he did. So the only thing Keith could conclude was that Edna had gotten involved herself somehow and had either carried on where Richard left off or carried did out her own investigations. Edna had been thrown out of church when she came to live with them. There had to be a connection there somehow. And the thing Keith found truly horrifying and unbelievable was the way things were around here lately, with Rebecca refusing to let anyone in that room because Edna had accomplished whatever she set out to do.

From the moment Keith discovered the real identity to Santa Claus, the Tooth Fairy, and all the other illustrious fake characters from his childhood, he refused to believe in anything that couldn't be proven one way or the other. This policy had followed him into adulthood and may have been partly the reason he enjoyed working with numbers. Numbers could be manipulated, yes, but when added together—or their parts subtracted—they offered facts, something that could be written down and proven beyond a doubt. He didn't believe in ghosts, ghouls, aliens—although his mathematician's brain refused to accept they were alone in the universe—or the afterlife. When someone died, they became food for the bugs and worms, rotting away until nothing but bone remained, and nothing else. So, for this to be happening to both him and Ashley now beggared belief. It was impossible that what he was considering should be even feasible.

But the hairs on the back of his neck standing to attention were testament to the fact that he was seriously thinking about the possibility. That, plus the way Rebecca had looked at him while blatantly lying, knowing perfectly well he was telling the truth, made him sit up and think about his options. And what exactly were they?

That morning, on the way to his office, he had heard about another desecration at Bradwell Cemetery on the radio. Something else he found horrific and disturbing—for what possible reason would anyone want to do such a thing? According to the police, an organ had been taken from the deceased body and police were looking for suspects. Had some satanic cult been operating in the area again like a few years ago? Was it kids? He didn't know, but now that he was all alone in the privacy of his office, anger was the emotion rapidly taking over from fear and disbelief.

That woman had been a bitch in life and even now that she was dead, she was still causing them problems. If, *if*, somehow, she had found a way to come back as a rather spiteful ghost, short of calling a priest to do some kind of exorcism or blessing or whatever they did nowadays—which would surely alert all the neighbours, causing immense embarrassment should word get out—there also had to be a way to send her back. And he thought there just might be a way to find out if all this was real or not. Because, if he did a little digging—both physically and metaphorically-speaking—and nothing was wrong it would mean it was time to take himself and Ash to Northgate Hospital for the Mentally Impaired for an extended visit, for suffering severe hallucinations. If his suspicions were confirmed though it meant Edna really had discovered the secret to life after death.

Keith glanced at his watch. It was almost nine in the evening and he'd barely done a thing all day. He'd already told Rebecca he had to work late to finish a client's tax returns so he could just as easily text her to say the client had insisted on taking him for a drink afterwards. It happened often, so she wouldn't suspect anything, but there were two other problems. One of which was slightly less significant than the other, but he couldn't live like this, knowing he might wake up in that godforsaken bedroom again. Or worse, get thrown into the wardrobe, never to be seen again. Or that it happened to Ash, because he seemed to be the one being targeted here. Karl hadn't said a thing.

Keith wasn't a particularly spontaneous person, preferring to deliberate matters, but this was not a normal situation. Besides, if he thought about it too much, he knew he would back out of this mad idea of his. He grabbed his stuff, turned off the computer, and headed out of his office before he could change his mind.

First, he headed towards home but stopped at the top of the street and hurried to the garage at the bottom of the garden, knowing that Rebecca would be watching TV and probably getting the kids ready for bed. He found and grabbed what he needed then rushed back out before she or anyone else saw him. Back in his car, he drove to Bradwell Cemetery. This was where the larger of his problems might arise. Grabbing a shovel had been the lesser one.

Given that there had been two desecrations in less than a week that might mean there would be police surveillance around the area. But given it was a small village with a relatively small force, he didn't think their budget included 24-hour stakeouts. What it might include was an officer driving around the area every now and again as part of their shift, so he would have to be fast. And he didn't suppose the vicar would be up all night patrolling the grounds either, considering his age. So Keith willed his heart to slow down a little bit and hurried to the fence, throwing the shovel over the gate. He climbed up and landed with a thud in the graveyard, his heart immediately performing nervous jigs in his chest again.

The last time he had been in a graveyard at night was when he was a half drunken teenager with friends. Looking around him now, he saw large branches blowing gently in the breeze that could have easily been mistaken as the arms of some ghoulish creature lurking about. An owl sitting in a tree stared at him, its eyes golden and huge. Rustling near a small bush could be anything.

He shook his head. It was impressive what having a semi-dead mother-in-law in one's life could conjure in one's mind—assuming his worst suspicions were true. Bad enough when mothers-in-law were alive and normal, let alone come back from the dead trying to drag you into the wardrobe for all eternity.

Not wanting to waste time procrastinating on the matter, he headed to the woman's grave. Fortunately, the moon was full, providing him with enough light to perform the job at hand. It also showed him how Edna's death affected everything else around her. The grass around her grave was brown, dry and dead, in stark contrast to the rest of the graves. The flowers nearby were wilted and drooping. Even the headstone seemed older than it should be, moss already growing thick, the headstone discoloured as if it had been here centuries rather than a few weeks. The pigeons and other assorted birdlife must also have taken a dislike to her, or sensed something was wrong, because it was pretty much the only headstone covered in bird droppings.

Keith took another quick look around and started digging, still wondering what the hell he was doing but trying to keep a picture of Edna dragging him into the wardrobe as a reminder of his madness. The ground wasn't as hard as he had expected, either, but it was still tough work. He was used to pushing pens, shaking hands, and typing on laptops, not doing things that might cause a hernia. But he pushed on, ignoring the rustling in bushes, squeaks and squawks from the nocturnal creatures hunting for food. He also tried to ignore the stabbing sensation in his back and kidneys, but this was tougher. He had already developed a beer gut from too many client sessions at the pub. Keith vowed that once this was over, it was time to sign up at the local gym.

He didn't think he was even halfway down yet when he needed a break, the sweat dripping into his eyes, making them sting. A stitch in his side made him wince with each laboured breath. He still hadn't thought about how he was going to open the coffin. In the films, they hacked at it with a shovel or a crowbar, but didn't they have simple latches nowadays? Just flip it open like a normal box? He was beginning to regret this already and he'd only just started. He must have been mad thinking he could just come in here, dig up a coffin, and see if there was a body in there or not. And that was another thing; how badly would Edna have decomposed by now, after 4 weeks? He'd already been having nightmares about her coming for him in the dead of night. What if he opened that coffin and a new layer of nightmares were revealed to him? Edna covered in maggots and worms, her flesh dripping off her like fat on a Sunday roast, showing parts of her skeleton beneath. Eyeballs like golf balls staring up at him, perhaps starting to cave in on themselves or even completely missing. No, he hadn't thought this out properly at all.

But it was too late to back away now.

Aware that he couldn't arrive home too late— the pubs closed at eleven—or Rebecca would start getting worried, he resumed digging, gritting his teeth against the pain in his side and the stinging of his eyes. After another fifteen minutes or so, the shovel finally clinked against something hard. Keith let out a gasp of relief, as he was starting to believe the old witch had been buried about two hundred foot down or something, well out of harm's way. With renewed vigour, he started frantically removing the last of the soil until he saw the outline of the cheap coffin.

"Stop what the hell you are doing and turn around slowly."

Keith's heart almost exploded in his chest. His body froze, paralysed with shock and fear. He dropped the shovel and did as he was told. "Look, this isn't what you think. I wa—"

"Shut up. It's exactly what I think it is. Tell me, you were gonna take that poor woman's heart as well? Then what, eat it? Like that sick Dahmer guy? Turn around and put your hands behind your back. You're under arrest, sicko."

The burly policeman shining the torch in his face wasn't going to listen to him. He thought about climbing out and running, trying his luck, but his legs ached. Also, he still had a stitch and didn't think he would get very far before collapsing. If he did and the cop caught him, he would probably beat the hell out of Keith for trying. But unless he did something, and fast, this kind of trouble just might destroy his life and that of everyone around him.

"Listen, please. I had nothing to do with those other desecrations. This is my mother-in-law's grave and—"

"What?! Wasn't enough to dig up a stranger's grave, you had to go and dig up your mother-in-law's as well? What kind of sick pervert are you? You got mummy issues or something? Get your hands behind your back or I'll break them."

Keith couldn't see the officer too well with the bright beam in his face, but he could see the truncheon. The only good thing about this was that he wasn't in America or he might have been shot by now as well.

He had no choice except hope that at the station, he could try and explain his situation with a less nervous officer and pray they believed him. Get

Rebecca to back him up as well. And then it occurred to him that the reasons behind his actions were very probably far less believable than admitting to being a graverobber. For the first time since Karl was born, Keith wanted to cry.

Chapter

16

Rebecca had been asleep on the sofa when he got home. She woke up and the questions started. Hopefully the kids, still asleep upstairs, would remain ignorant of all this.

"Are you stupid?! What were you thinking?"

Normally, Keith might have responded to his wife that yes, it was stupid, but he wasn't going to give her that satisfaction. What he had been thinking was partly her fault anyway; that was why he had decided to dig up her mother.

"What I was thinking, Rebecca, is that the other night I got dragged into that hellish bedroom your mother died in and then into her wardrobe. I was also thinking about Ashley being dragged from his bed and taken into that room. You saw the marks around his ankle as well as I did. And you also know full well it wasn't no nightmare we both had, either. You're hiding something about Edna, and I wanna know what.

I went to her grave last night because I wanted to make sure she was in it."

"Are you listening to yourself? I'm not surprised the police wanted to keep you there. Christ, I'm also surprised they didn't send you straight away to Northgate and throw away the key. You are seriously suggesting that my mother is not dead? That somehow she is still alive, locked away in her bedroom, and occasionally decides to creep out at night and drag both you and Ashley back in there? It's nuts, Keith! Nuts! You saw her when she died. Saw her body being carted away in a body bag. Have you started taking drugs or something?"

"Yeah, me and your twelve-year-old son have started taking acid a few nights a week. A few magic mushrooms, as well. For God's sake, explain to me why it is so important to you that no one goes in that room? Why you felt the need to put a lock on the door and were about to send Ash and Karl to your sister's for a month? If Edna is dead, why all the secrecy?"

"Because… I wanted to keep the room as it was. I didn't want the kids going through her old junk. I just wanted her forgotten about."

"Why?"

"Because she was a witch! I didn't want the kids stumbling on any of that crap she used to read or anything."

"So why not just empty her room, throw everything out?"

"Because I didn't. But don't you go making this about me. You're the one who tried to dig her grave up, not me. I wasn't as stupid as you. I—"

Rebecca spun away, her cheeks suddenly flushed.

In that moment, Keith was barely aware. He was probably red-faced himself and definitely tired as hell, wanting nothing more than to go to bed. But he was determined that before he did so, he got some answers. The police had wanted them too and, while sitting there in a cell for what seemed like weeks, he had thought about what he was going to say. If he told them the truth—or what he thought to be the truth—Rebecca was right; they would have carted him off in a straitjacket. Instead, he came up with a story about believing to have dropped his wedding ring in her coffin at the funeral and wanted it back before his wife found out.

The detective, a Tom Riddley, had stared at him as though he was mad, a flicker of a grin on his face. *You really expect me to believe that?*

Keith had insisted it was true (after earlier hiding the real ring in his pocket) and that he was pretty sure he had alibis for the previous desecrations and he had absolutely no need for dead people's hearts. He also mentioned he had two young sons as if this would prove he wasn't some ghoulish, monstrous figure prowling the streets at night. The detective reminded him that John Wayne Gacy and Dennis

Rader, among others, also had families. To that Keith had no answers. He was formally charged and told to expect a visit in the next few days.

"You still haven't explained to me properly what's going on, Rebecca. If it had just happened to Ash, I would have said the same thing—nightmares and curiosity got the better of him. But it happened to me as well. It all sounds just as crazy to me as it would to anyone else, but I know what I felt and saw. I also know there are things you haven't told me about your mother, but she got kicked out of church and was dabbling in some black magic crap. And now, a month later, two of us have started seeing and hearing her, not to mention getting dragged into her locked room. So, for your kid's sakes, I suggest you figure out whatever it is that's going on and make it stop, before you wake up one morning and your kids are gone. Or worse yet, dead!"

"Well, maybe I'll explain everything to the judge when you're in court accused of stealing organs! The kids will love that! I should have known trouble would come of it. What was I thinking?"

This woman was as stubborn as her mother. She was hiding something and was prepared to risk her children's sanity to protect that knowledge? He recalled with vivid clarity hearing Edna in her room at nights chanting occasionally in English, sometimes in another language that sounded remarkably like Latin or some obscure, ancient tongue. It drove Keith mad.

Rebecca always had a look in her eye that oozed fear and loathing, too, but she never tried to make her stop. Instead, she would turn the radio or the TV up louder, until it became too much to bear. Then she would rush upstairs, and the screaming matches would start. Even Ashley, who was just a baby back then, would suddenly burst out crying for no reason, even when he was fast asleep, as though he could sense the horrors occurring upstairs. When Keith asked his wife what Edna was doing, Rebecca always gave him the same reply—she's going senile in her old age, remembering stuff from when she lived in the mansion. Keith never really believed her then and he most certainly didn't now.

"I don't know, Rebecca. What are you thinking? I just spent the night at a police station. Unless the charges are dropped, I will end up in court accused of graverobbing. My clients are gonna love that if it gets out—which it probably will—and I may therefore be out of a job. So why don't you help out a little and tell me what is going on?"

"It's your own stupid fault for going to her grave and trying to dig her up! Right after the last two, as well, so you had to know there would be police cars patrolling the area. Christ, how stupid can you get? You didn't see me getting caught. I…"

Rebecca's jaw dropped. She froze, cheeks blushing bright red.

"What did you just say?" asked Keith.

Before she could answer, there was banging and laughter coming from upstairs. The kids were awake.

Chapter

17

Edna's Story

Six months had passed since Edna was refused a seat
at Richard's séance, but she hadn't been idle. Nor had
Richard, although this time it was because he had to go
away on a business trip. Edna couldn't have been
happier. Most of her time was spent attending to
Rebecca and making daily trips to Bradwell Cemetery
to visit Alison's grave, so she rarely saw her husband,
anyway. But the fact that he would be out of this house
for nearly five months was the best she could have
wished for.

She almost wept with relief when the chauffeur
arrived and took him away. She wouldn't have minded
if she never saw him again. Edna didn't know to what
country he was going—they had barely spoken a single
word to each other since Alison's death—but she
secretly hoped it was some far off third-world country
where he might succumb to a rare disease and die. Or
maybe a plane crash. Attacked and killed by some

rogue, rabid dog. Anything that would see him pay for what he did to their daughter. For no matter what he tried to tell her when Alison died, that it had been an accident, she refused to believe him. He'd only been to her grave twice since she died. Edna wondered if he'd forgotten already that she had ever lived. For the first time in her life, she knew what it meant to truly hate somebody. To wish them dead, that they would suffer like no other had ever suffered before. She would kill him herself if she thought she could summon the courage. Her mind and soul had turned black, consumed by a desire for revenge. If she cut herself, her blood would flow the colour of oil, dark as night, her heart a shrivelled thing in her chest, rotting and foul. If it wasn't for Rebecca, she might have already tried to kill her husband.

So, with the house to herself—except for Rebecca, the two maids, and the cook—she could resume what she had hoped to do all those months ago and contact the spirit of her daughter. It had tortured her, being unable to gain access to the Ouija board that Richard kept locked away. Often, at night when he finally headed off to sleep, she would rise and creep around the house searching for the key, but she knew Richard was aware of that and being sly. He kept the key in his pocket at all times. She suspected when he went to bed that he put the key under his pillow.

On one occasion, she dared to sneak in his room, knowing he had fallen asleep drunk and would therefore not wake up, and searched every single drawer, but found nothing. She had rummaged through his clothes, even pulling back the blanket to see if his pyjamas had pockets, but again, to no luck. Either he had a hidden, secret safe somewhere or that key never left his possession.

But now he was gone, and in his haste and stress at having to prepare his own suitcases, she thought and prayed he might have forgotten all about it.

And she was right.

The minute his chauffeur drove away, she rushed to his room and looked under the pillow. There it was, a tiny gold key that gave access to the cupboard in his study where he kept the board and planchette. She let out a little squeal of delight and snatched it up. And when she opened the cupboard in his study, took out the board and hugged it to her chest, it was as if she was hugging her baby daughter all over again.

After feeding Rebecca, who was already walking, much to the delight of the maids, happier than she had ever seen them since Richard left, she left Rebecca with them and hurried to her bedroom. She stared at the board on her writing desk with awe and excitement, like it was some ancient, mystical artifact she had just discovered. When she touched it, it was as if she'd just received a jolt of electricity, her fingers and spine tingling in anticipation. She ran her fingers gently over the planchette as if it were some pet—a kitten, perhaps—smiling as she considered how to use the object.

Edna recalled all the times she'd overheard Richard in his study and the things he'd said to summon the spirits. Had he asked for a particular spirit or just randomly asked them to appear? She couldn't quite remember now despite the multiple times she'd listened in. But really, it didn't matter. There was only one soul she wanted—*needed*—to contact. Maybe, if things went well, her blood and heart may not be tinged with hot rage any longer.

"Alison? Alison, are you there? It's me, your mother. Can you hear me?" she asked timidly, her fingers tracing the planchette in circles.

No sound came, no sudden twitching of the planchette. Warm tears trickled down her cheeks— whether from hearing her daughter's name again or the risk of disappointment, she didn't know.

She asked again, a twinge of impatience in her voice now. It didn't matter; she would stay here all day until Alison answered. She had to know where she was and if she was okay. If Richard was right, after all, or not.

"Alison? Please, it's me. Let me know if you are here. If you're okay. Mummy's worried about you."

She looked around her bedroom for a sign. A shadow over in the corner, a twitching of the curtains or rustling from somewhere, but there was nothing.

She focused on the planchette, willing it to move, then moved it herself, as though trying to encourage it to spell out some signal. When this failed, her face crumbled, lips quivering with despair and grief, wondering if she would ever hear her daughter's voice again, or possibly see her.

Then it happened.

At first, she assumed it had been her that inadvertently caused the planchette to twitch. But when it spelled out the word 'hello', a gasp of delight escaped her. In her shock, she almost sent the thing flying across the room.

"Alison, is that you?! Please tell me it is."

The planchette moved to 'yes'.

"Oh my God. It's really you? This isn't some kind of prank? Can you prove to me it's really you?"

For what seemed like an eternity, enough for Edna to believe this was indeed a prank, nothing happened. Then she noticed movement out the corner of her eye. She turned and gasped again, a hand flying to her mouth, hard enough to sting her lips. Over in the far corner of the room, something barely visible flickered. She could see the wall through it, almost like a thin sheet flapping in the wind. Then, it gradually formed into the small outline of a child and Edna recognised immediately the long, black hair flowing out behind her as though underwater and the green eyes that sparkled like emeralds. Even though it was faint and the figure semi-transparent, it was Alison who smiled timidly, wearing the long, flowery dress she had been buried in.

Edna was openly sobbing now, wanting to rush to her daughter and hug her. Yet, at the same time, she didn't want to ruin the moment, cause her daughter's spirit to disappear again. She had to force herself to remain seated, so many questions running through her mind that she didn't know where to start.

"I miss you, Alison. And…and your sister is so big now! She's walking and talking already, such a handful. Much more than you ever were! And…and tell me Alison, are you in Heaven? Did you go to Heaven, but can come back when I call you with the board?"

Alison shook her head. Her smile faded.

"Then…then where are you?"

Alison circled the air. *Everywhere.*

"But can't you move on? Why can't you go to Heaven?"

A voice, barely audible as though coming from a great distance played softly in Edna's ear. "Can't go. Not yet. Not allowed."

"Not allowed? But why? Who says you can't move on? G-God?"

She shook her head. "Daddy."

"Daddy? Daddy won't let you move on? But how is that possible? He's here on Earth. He's not here in this house—he's away on business—but how can he stop you from moving on?"

"Daddy is bad. He did this."

Edna's heart dropped into her stomach. She had known deep down all along that Richard had wanted vengeance on her for refusing to play out his fantasies, but to kill their own daughter? A part of her still refused to believe the man, or anyone, could be capable of such a thing. But now, here was the confirmation.

"What did he do, Alison? Did he push you down the stairs?"

She nodded.

If Richard was here, in this house right this very second, she wouldn't have needed to find any amount of courage. She would have grabbed a knife and stabbed him to death there and then. Now more than ever, she wanted to embrace her daughter, hug her tight to her chest and tell her she was sorry for what he did. That he would pay for it. But this wasn't going to make the shimmering figure in the corner come to life.

"He will pay, Alison. I promise. His idea of dying and coming back again is only going to half work. He won't be coming back here as himself or as anyone else. I will ensure that. Tell me, baby, what is it like where you are? Is it at least a happy place?"

Again, the girl shook her head. "No, it's a horrible, scary place. So cold and dark, and there are…things here with me. Scary things that want to hurt me. I don't like it here. I want to leave, but they won't let me."

A haunting wail echoed around the bedroom, seeming to come from behind the walls, under the floorboards, in Edna's skull. She wanted to die herself, go to her daughter and protect her. It wasn't enough that the girl's own father had deliberately killed her, but that Alison's current residence was a place of horror was the final straw. There wasn't even any peace in the belief the girl was in a happy place as Edna had been telling herself all this time.

"Who wants to hurt you, Alison? Be strong. I promise I will make things better again."

She was thinking of dragging Mary over here to do another séance, this time without Richard. Surely she could contact Alison and whatever spirit was hurting her and make them stop?

"Bad things, Mummy. I think they're demons. I can't see their faces, but they have huge bodies and lots of arms and legs. And teeth. They're coming now! I have to go. Help me, Mummy!"

The last word faded away, as did Alison. Edna jumped up and screamed for her daughter to come back, to run away. She howled and yelled at these creatures to leave her baby alone, picking up the planchette and throwing it at the wall. She picked up the Ouija board too, planning on snapping it in half, but a distant voice in her head, like a part of her subconscious, warned her against it. She would need it later, the voice told her. Already she had a plan in her mind, and an old friend of Richard's was going to be the one to help her. For that, she would certainly need the Ouija board.

Chapter

18

It was almost Ashley's thirteenth birthday, and he should have been excited. Finally becoming a teenager, on the cusp of adulthood, yet the last thing on his mind was parties and birthdays and presents. Right now, he couldn't care less if he was about to celebrate his first or his fiftieth. Normally, his parents—especially his dad—would have been teasing him, asking how it felt to be an adult, an old man. If he was going to invite him to a beer down at the pub, get a job. Marry his secret girlfriend. But they seemed to have entirely forgotten about the whole thing. Not even Karl had started on him yet, which was so unlike him as well.

His birthday was just three days away and it might as well have been three months. Ashley didn't even care. What he did care about was the argument between his parents that morning when he woke up. He had opened his eyes to hear his mother yelling, and she had said some things that caused Ashley to bolt upright and head to the bedroom door, where he opened it to quietly eavesdrop.

His initial reaction was that they were arguing about some film they'd watched the night before, or maybe something they'd seen on the news, because it didn't make sense. As far as he could make out, someone had got arrested for doing something in the local graveyard and Mum was furious. So was Dad. But there was also talk about Grandma and digging up coffins.

This was when he really started getting upset and nervous. If he was hearing them correctly, it had been Grandma's coffin someone had tried to get into. If someone had tried to open her coffin, it meant she was either a vampire or a zombie that wanted to kill. Then everything was true—she really was coming back from the grave to torment them. Ashley appeared to be her preferred victim. As he listened further, he was pretty sure Mum was accusing dad of being the one who had gone to her grave and he might have been caught—something about going to court and losing his job. But then, just as Ashley strained to hear more, Karl had come stumbling loudly from his room.

That was the end of that.

He had known from the beginning that something was definitely wrong concerning Grandma. That he hadn't imagined hearing her voice or getting dragged out of bed. He also knew Dad, and especially Mum, seemed to be hiding something. When Dad saw the mark on his ankle, Ashley had been sure he was about to reveal some secret about Grandma, but then he suddenly shut up. All this time, Ashley believed it was Grandma's ghost haunting him, which, while scary—and being dragged into her room was proof of that—ghosts couldn't really do anything much worse than that, could they, except drag him out of bed a few times? Wasn't as if her ghost was going to come and eat him one night while he lay in bed asleep. But now, if she was indeed some kind of ghoul, this changed everything. Now his life was in danger, not just his sanity.

He'd just got home from school and this argument had been on his mind all day, to the point several teachers had yelled at him for not paying attention in class. He didn't care about that. Let them phone his parents and tell them. What were they going to say? *Yeah, sorry about that. Ashley is in the process of being hunted and eaten by his dead grandmother, so he's a little worried right now*. Hardly. And this was what really broke his heart and made him want to cry—it was as if they didn't care. He couldn't understand how, after everything that had happened to him, his parents could still dismiss the whole thing as mere nightmares on his behalf. They had seen the laceration on his ankle, and Grandma's bedroom door had been wide open when only Mum had the key, so why weren't they doing anything to protect him? Did they *want* him to get taken? They should have gone to the police by now, or called a priest to exorcise his grandma. They had to do something to stop her, but whenever he tried to raise the subject with his mother, she fobbed him off with either not having time to discuss it or simply telling him to 'shut up, for God's sake, with all that nonsense.'

Why him and not Karl? This was another question. He sat in his bedroom, slouched on the bed looking up at the ceiling, and understanding nothing. The tears came again. His parents barely even spoke to him anymore, just a mumbled 'how's school?' and 'have you done your homework?' Aside from the argument that morning, they barely talked to each other. Ashley had never known the house to be so quiet. At the weekends, they would usually pile into the car and go to the country if it was warm and sunny. Perhaps Dad might take him to a football match, even. But since Grandma had died none of that happened anymore. It was as if something died in this household along with the old woman.

Except now, Grandma wasn't really dead, was she?

He had a feeling that soon, maybe even this very night, she might return for him and take him away. For good.

At school, he had told his best friend, Kevin, nothing, not wanting to be the butt of everyone's joke. But he had suggested Kevin might come over for the night. It was Saturday tomorrow, which meant no school, and Kevin used to stay over quite regularly. They would hit the PlayStation until the early hours and snack on pizza and biscuits. Kevin didn't have a PlayStation, so this was a perfect reason for him to come to Ashley's and not the other way around. Usually on those nights, Karl would do the opposite. He'd go stay at his own friend's, so he didn't have to worry about the little brat being a nuisance.

"Mum, is it okay if Kevin stays over tonight?"

She was sitting on the sofa reading a book, but he'd noticed she'd been on the same page for at least five minutes, staring absently. She looked older now, too. Strands of grey were starting to appear in her hair and there were wrinkles around her eyes that hadn't been there a week ago. She looked as though she might have aged twenty years. When she cooked their dinner, it was just the same boring old thing—in fact, these last few weeks it had consisted mostly of pizza and pre-cooked meals to shove in a microwave. Before, she always prided herself on her cooking, and nobody questioned her abilities for good reason.

"Mmm?" she asked not even acknowledging his presence.

"I said, can Kevin stay over for the night? I have to phone him to let him know."

"What? Oh, umm… Oh, I don't know. I mean, your father and I have a lot to discuss later, but…but yeah, what the hell. Okay, yes, he can. You'll be in your room all night, won't you?"

"Yeah, of course."

"Okay, fine. I'll order pizzas then for supper."

Ashley thanked her and left.

As he headed up the stairs and glanced into the open living room, his mother was staring absently ahead, frowning. The idea that maybe Mum was going slightly senile, like his grandmother had, sent shivers down his spine. Maybe he was going senile, too, for believing Grandma might be a vampire.

Usually, having Kevin over was a great source of excitement. They'd stay up until their eyes could handle it no longer, laughing and joking as they played game after game of football on the PlayStation, munching on biscuits and chocolate until they were nearly sick. But as the night wore on, Ashley wasn't feeling steadily sicker from chocolate but from nerves.

It was hard work, but Ashley managed to act as if nothing was wrong and pretended to be enjoying the football matches as always. When his eyes started to sting and the yawning began, his thoughts turned to what was to come. But he was confident that by having Kevin in the same room as him, it would dissuade Grandma from coming in should she decide to do so. Ashley might lose the ability to scream at the top of his lungs, but Kevin sure as hell wouldn't. Kevin was scared of anything and everything.

Eventually, after Ashley's parents came up and told them not to stay up too late, the battle to stay awake themselves was lost around 1 a.m. They both crawled into bed, which fortunately was big enough for the both of them and within minutes Ashley fell asleep feeling less nervous than he had in weeks. His plan was going to work. At least for tonight.

Kevin should have known this would happen. really, it was his own fault. But before they had climbed into bed, he hadn't needed the toilet. Not at all. Hadn't even crossed his mind, even when Ashley had gone. But now, in the middle of the night, Kevin's bladder felt like it was going to explode if he didn't do something about it and quick. And if he happened to piss in Ashley's bed somehow, it would be all over school come Monday morning. Ashley's brother Karl would ensure of that, no worries.

The biggest problem Kevin faced was that he was terrified of the dark. The idea of running to the toilet across the landing in the pitch black was something he wouldn't usually do in his own home, let alone a friend's. He could turn on the lamp beside the bed, but that would awaken Ashley, and he might not be too happy about that. He'd been acting moody and bad-tempered lately as it was, anyway. There was no way he was going to risk struggling to find a light switch on the landing and waking Ashley's mum. She had a bad temper sometimes as well. He'd heard her scolding Ashley for the most trivial things on occasion, so if he inadvertently woke her now, she might get really angry.

Uh-huh. Not gonna happen.

But he had to do something or wetting Ashley's bed would see him in very serious trouble in the morning. He had no choice but to risk the lesser of two evils. If he was really fast, he could make it to their toilet without tripping or falling down the stairs and be back again within seconds.

He glanced at Ashley, who was snoring softly, his back to him. Kevin doubted he would wake up. Then, as quietly as possible, Kevin climbed out of bed. He opened the bedroom door and peered out. It could have been miles to the toilet. It was so dark out there that he couldn't see a thing. But he knew it was directly at the top of the stairs, slightly to the right, so all he had to do was fumble his way along the wall on his left then head to the right at the end. Easy. He tried to mentally recall any obstacles that might be in the way—a small table or something, one of Karl's shoes—and realised it didn't matter anyway if he tripped and made loads of noise. His bladder was going to open up at any second.

He made it.

Barely, but he found the bathroom without falling down the stairs, and unleashing the contents of his bladder was pure bliss. He cursed himself for being such a baby and idiot and for putting himself through so much trauma. When he finished, he pulled the chain and left, ready to dash back to the safety of the bedroom. But as he left, he abruptly stopped. For one thing, he could see quite clearly the landing which hadn't been the case ten seconds ago. The door next to Ashley's was wide open, and there was a beam of moonlight shining out onto the landing.

His worst fears ran through his mind. He had indeed woken Ashley's mum and now she was waiting for him, ready to strangle him for daring to wake her in the middle of the night.

Darn.

Sheepishly, he made his way back, trying to think of a decent apology.

A shadow flickered back and forth in that room. Was she going to jump out at him, try and scare him as well for what he did? That was a little exaggerated, wasn't it? All he had done was go to the toilet.

He made it to the open door, almost cringing at what was to come, when the shadow moved suddenly to the left, out of sight.

"Kevin, come here," came a soft whisper.

Jesus, he thought. Was his friend's mum really that strict? Ashley had told him about his aunt and how religious and strict she was, and Kevin has seen his mother in action sometimes, screaming at him for the slightest of things, like forgetting to do his homework, but this? What the hell was she going to do to him in there? But regardless, he went in, not wanting to upset her any further. The door slowly closed of its own accord, and he found himself in an empty bedroom with a large wardrobe, its doors wide open too. The room was hot and stuffy, as if the windows hadn't been opened in weeks, and smelled of mildew and decay.

"Umm, sorry, Mrs. Rice. I didn't mean to wake you, I just needed the toilet real bad and—"

"Hush, Kevin. Come here."

Now it didn't quite sound like Ashley's mum. The voice had more of a croaky aspect to it, like his grandmother who had chain smoked for years until cancer killed her. He stepped into the room towards the wardrobe. Kevin was getting very scared. He had the absurd thought that she was going to drag him into the wardrobe and he would disappear, taken to another world like in Narnia, but this time, one much scarier.

A hand reached out from inside beckoning him. It was a huge, fat hand, fingers like pork sausages and covered in wrinkles, fingernails like claws. The hand outstretched for him to take it, which, despite his reluctance, he did. He gasped at how cold it was, then again when he was dragged forcefully into the wardrobe, not even having time to resist. Just before the doors slammed closed, the last thing he saw were two silver eyes—like twin moons—towering over him. He also had time to notice the smell of old flowers and the stench of rot before a cold, clammy hand wrapped itself around his throat and he was barely aware he'd just released the contents of his bladder. Or his bowels.

"I can't find him anywhere, I said!" yelled Ashley in desperation.

His parents sat up in bed, looks of annoyance on their faces.

"Well, maybe he went home early without telling you, Ash, for God's sake! What is it with you lately?" said his mother.

"His clothes are here, I'm telling you. So is his phone. Why would he go home in his pyjamas without his phone?"

That did the trick. Ten minutes later, after frantically calling and searching the whole house and going out into the street to call for him as well, they had to concede that Kevin was gone. They had no choice but to call Kevin's parents and the police.

The boy's parents were the first to arrive. Ashley, in tears, had to listen to all the screaming and arguing, demanding to know what they had done with their son, what Ashley had done. But all he could tell them was the same thing over and over—he woke up and Kevin was nowhere to be found. His plan had backfired on him, for he was pretty sure he knew what had happened. The uneasy glances between his parents suggested they suspected the same thing.

When a detective arrived, he saw his father visibly groan and his shoulders slump. They all headed into the living room.

"I'm Detective Tom Riddley, but you already know that, so tell me what happened."

Kevin's parents were still sobbing and holding onto each other tightly. Ashley told the detective what he knew. Then his parents stated how they had searched the whole house and street and couldn't find him. They went to Ashley's bedroom and Kevin's mother cried uncontrollably when she saw her son's clothes on the floor, his phone on the table.

Tom radioed the station and shortly after, two female officers arrived. After some heated discussion, Kevin's parents were escorted back to their home, leaving the four of them plus Karl, who sat on the sofa looking terrified and nervous.

"Ashley, Karl, why don't you go to your rooms. We need to discuss something with the detective," said Rebecca.

Knowing there was no point in arguing, they trudged upstairs. But Ashley immediately crept halfway back down again so he could eavesdrop.

"So, you're going to tell me this is a coincidence, aren't you?" asked the detective.

"Yes!" replied Keith. "My wife and I were both asleep. We had no idea Kevin was missing. What are you suggesting?"

"I'm not suggesting anything. But first, you get arrested for trying to desecrate your mother-in-law's grave. Then, a few days later, a kid goes missing from your house while everyone's asleep. We have two other graves that have been desecrated, their organ's missing, so I dunno… Might make me think about some Devil worshipping thing going on."

"That's ridiculous. You want to search my whole house, go ahead. See if you can find black robes and masks and books on Devil worshipping. Good luck with that."

They continued chatting for a while, until the detective evidently decided they weren't going to confess to murder or anything else. He told them he would be in touch and left.

Ashley rushed upstairs again before he was caught, but still heard his father's comment as soon as he closed the door. "So, Rebecca, you ready to tell me what the hell is going on? Why don't we look in your mother's wardrobe? Because I'm pretty sure that was the last place Ash's friend was before disappearing."

Rebecca said nothing.

Chapter

19

Edna's story

The world Edna inhabited revolved purely and solely around her husband. As though he was the centre of her universe but had become trapped in a black hole residing in her mind that she was unable to escape. She saw him in her sleep, while playing with Rebecca, while wandering aimlessly through the many corridors of her house, as though he were a ghost stalking her. His voice echoed throughout the house, in her head. His chuckling like the laughter of the Devil himself made her cringe and want to crawl somewhere and die. He was her nemesis, haunting her twenty-four hours of the day. Especially that look he'd had in his eyes as she cradled Alison at the bottom of the stairs. Only recently there had been a scandal in the country after it was discovered retired doctor, John Christie, had murdered several women, even allowing another, innocent man to be hung for those crimes. Richard had had that same look in his eyes as when Christie was

arrested and brought before justice—a psychopath's
eyes.

And right now, she was his current victim.

Three weeks had passed since Edna's discovery
about Alison and the tears had barely stopped falling.
She spent hours each day at the cemetery with
Rebecca, chatting to Alison, telling her of her plans.
But Alison never returned in spirit form, despite
Edna's insistence. This only fuelled her hatred towards
Richard and his obsessions. So when she received
news that he would be coming home early—in the next
few days, in fact—she was sad that he hadn't died
somehow. Then it was time to prepare for his arrival.

She had got into the habit of returning the key
to his pillow each night after using the board so that
when he did come home, she wouldn't ruin everything
by having forgotten. Richard would kill her if he found
out she had been using it without his knowledge or
permission. For what she hoped would be the final
time, she grabbed the board again and took it to the
privacy of her bedroom. The planchette had been
destroyed when she threw it at the wall the last time.
Fortunately, she had found an antique store in town
that had something almost, if not exactly, similar.

She took the board and sat on the bed. Candles
dotted around the room that she found helped to settle
her mind.

"It's me again. Are you there?"

She waited patiently for a reply. She had come to learn that sometimes it took longer than other times for contact to be established. On several occasions, the spirit had appeared immediately. Others, after more than fifteen minutes, as if the spirit was far away and needed to make the long journey physically to contact her. This time, after asking for just the third time, the flames from the candles flickered and there was a rustling of the curtain.

Edna smiled.

"Is that you? Have you answered my call?"

The planchette moved to yes.

"Good to see you again! Do you know why I called for you?"

No.

"He's coming home. You remember what I told you? What you told us? I want my revenge. I want him to pay for what he did. Are you going to help me?"

Yes.

"Thank you, Dorothy. This is what we are going to do…"

Two days later, Richard came home. He offered barely a mumble as he walked in the house, not looking his wife in the eyes, not asking about Rebecca, despite the girl hugging her mother's waist. Rebecca didn't seem to recognise him as her father anymore, treating him as though he was a stranger. He headed straight to his study while his chauffeur brought in his suitcases. Normally, she would have ignored him, pretend he wasn't there, but there was a rage coursing through her veins, consuming her, that made her body shake and her heart violently pulse against her ribcage. If Rebecca hadn't been with her, she might have gone and grabbed the biggest kitchen knife she could find right there and then.

Patience, she told herself. *All in good time.* Rebecca must never know, never understand what was to happen or why. Maybe when she was older some understanding of her mother's actions could be given, but not now. Not for a long time.

Edna returned to her room and spent the day with her only daughter. She knew that the first thing Richard would do would be return to his board. The day he returned from abroad, he was exhausted and apparently still had lots of business discussions to do. So he spent almost all afternoon on the phone with his associates. But the next day, after lunch, Edna watched from a distance as he stepped into his study and locked the door behind him. It was time.

Rebecca had been given to one of the maids, told to spend the day at the park, the fair, whatever she liked. She gave the maid a generous amount of money to do so, leaving just Edna and Richard. Edna crept along the corridor until she stood outside the study as she had so many times before.

"Is there anybody there? It's been a long time, but I hope you haven't all left. Please show yourselves if you are present," he began.

There was silence for a while except a tapping sound. She knew it was Richard impatiently drumming his fingers on the table.

"Please, tell me someone is there. I've missed you. Show yourself to me."

Then, through the glass panel in the door, she saw movement, a flickering, like a shadow darting past. She heard him gasp, perhaps in relief at being answered.

"Who are you? What is your name?"

There came a muffled whisper, like a gust of wind through a crack in the wall that she couldn't understand.

"Who? I don't understand. Why don't you reveal yourself to me more clearly? I wish to speak with you, ask you questions." said Richard.

"You know who I am," came the voice, more clearly. "You've always known. I have things to show you."

There was a click as the study door slowly unlocked itself and swung open. Edna rushed to hide near the basement beside the stairs. A shadowy figure, dark and semi-transparent floated out, its form that of a human but not defined enough to determine who. Edna thought she knew, though.

Richard followed the figure out into the hallway. "Where are you taking me? Tell me your name."

"All in good time," replied the spirit in a raspy, croaked voice.

It manoeuvred along the hallway until it came to the basement door which swung open on its own. Edna watched from her crouching position a little further ahead as Richard approached, frowning, not knowing where he was being led. This was the critical moment, getting him to go down there. It was pitch black down there, and Edna wasn't sure the man had even set foot in the place before, saying it was filthy and full of bugs. On one occasion, he'd locked a maid down there all night because she had dropped a bottle of his favourite scotch.

"You want answers," said the spirit. "The answers are all down there. Everything."

"The answers? What could possibly be down there? This is a prank or something? You're trying to trick me?"

"No trick. Only answers to your eternal questions. Another resides down there, who will have your answers. All of them."

A grin slowly formed on Richard's face. The man who had murdered his own daughter out of spite because Edna refused to participate in his plans took a step closer to the steps.

He found a light switch and flicked it on lighting up the room in an orange glow. But just before he was about to go down the wooden steps, Edna, hiding opposite them behind a door and watching through the crack, saw the spirit change. Richard had his back to it, but Edna grinned as the form took on a clearer structure, as though a real person revealing the dress she had been wearing when Richard killed her, her long, black hair blowing as if a strong wind had got up. She turned to face Edna, somehow knowing where she was, and Dorothy grinned.

Edna grinned back and dared to come out of her hiding place. She stood beside Dorothy and tapped Richard on the back.

He jumped, surprised, and turned around, still with a big, stupid smile on his face. It disappeared immediately when he recognised Dorothy standing there fully formed as though a real-life person herself. "Wh-what is it? Dorothy? Edna, what is going on?"

But Edna didn't have time to respond even if she had wanted to. She watched in amazement and awe as Dorothy's features changed. It was like watching someone age fifty years in less than ten seconds. The hair on her head turned grey and fell in clumps, leaving a bald scalp and just a few strands of hair like old cobwebs. Her skin turned the same dark shade of grey, wrinkling as it did so, until the skin fell off of her like confetti. It was followed by lumps of flesh. First, her cheeks dropped, exposing cheekbones. Her lips drooped and dangled by a thin sliver of flesh before falling, exposing rotting, black teeth. These, too, fell one by one. Within seconds, all that remained of Dorothy's face were two dead eyes, completely white, set deep in her eye sockets, while the rest of her face was a grinning skull, just the odd lump of flesh remaining. It had been like watching a person's face melt off.

The rest of her body followed suit until there was a large pile of flesh at her feet and the injuries sustained when Richard had pushed her were still clear to see—limbs twisted and bent out of shape at all the wrong places, a large crack in her skull where she must have banged her head upon impact. She was chuckling softly while all this took place, now nothing more than a skeletal figure pointing one withered, bony finger at Richard.

"Remember me, darling Richard?" she croaked. "I told you I'd show you answers and I will."

His mouth moved, as if trying to summon the strength to answer her, his eyes wide and bulging like Dorothy's were, flicking to Edna and Dorothy as if seeking answers to the horrors he was witnessing.

"You will discover all the answers you need first hand while you scream in Hell, because that is where you are going."

"You evil man," said Edna. "You killed my baby daughter out of spite. I would have killed you earlier myself if I had the chance and nerve, but Dorothy offered to help instead. I hope you rot in Hell, Richard Rice. You deserve all that and more."

With a simple prod of Edna's finger against Richard's chest, he was suddenly sent flying down the stairs, not stopping until there was a resounding crack as his head smashed into the concrete floor below. But he still wasn't dead. He groaned feebly as the blood began to pool beneath him.

Edna walked down the steps to watch his last moments. The final, personal touch she would add herself, if necessary. When she reached him, he raised a hand as if begging for help. She kicked it away in disgust. His other arm was much like Dorothy's, broken at the elbow, which she thought a perfect example of poetic justice. She chuckled.

Dorothy came to join her, now as her previous self, and she too smiled, although there was a deep sadness in her eyes.

"Help me" whimpered Richard.

"The Devil will help you, Richard. The Devil and all his servants. You wanted death. We gave it to you. And you will not return again in the body of another or as a spirit. Your death will be your end on this Earth. What was it you used to say to me? Oh yes, I remember now. 'The life of man is barely a whisper in the screaming void of time'. Well, you can scream for all eternity now, dear. And the only one who will hear you is Satan!"

With Richard still mumbling incoherencies, blood running from his mouth, the floor around him thick and sticky as it spread out, she sat and stared into his eyes as the life was drained from him. "Goodbye, Richard. The demons await you."

She picked up an old sheet from a chair next to him, folded it a few times, and covered his face, pressing down hard around his nostrils. Richard gurgled and choked, tried to push it off, but he was too weak to do so. After a couple of minutes, his arm flapped back down and he breathed his last.

"Good riddance," she said, and started crying.

Dorothy slowly vanished from sight while Edna collected the sheet to burn so there would be no evidence later to incriminate her.

Chapter

20

It was her own fault. She knew that now. No matter how much she tried to tell herself otherwise. Her subconscious had told her it had all been Keith's fault, for being so stupid and almost ruining everything. How he could even consider going to the cemetery in the middle of the night and digging up Edna's grave was complete madness. No one in their right mind would do such a thing, especially given the police were monitoring the place on a regular basis since the desecrations occurred. And if he had managed to dig up her body, what had he expected to find? The coffin empty? Then what would he have done? Call the vicar in to perform a blessing, an exorcism? They would be laughed out of the village.

All of this would have utterly destroyed her plans, set in place so many years ago when suspicion finally turned to belief. Rebecca had been so careful to ensure things went exactly according to the script she and Caroline had prepared when Edna refused to stop with her own plans. Things were set in motion. There was a set of events that needed to play out before she could put a stop to this, and Keith had nearly blown it all by getting himself arrested.

And yet…yes, it was her fault. She couldn't and shouldn't expect her husband, and especially Ashley, to think it was all a result of nightmares and paranoia. They deserved more than that, and she lived terrified that one day she would wake up and Ashley would be gone. Or Keith, if he continued messing around where he shouldn't. But she couldn't tell them that, of course. They would have her committed to Northgate if she revealed what was really going on.

Yet, if this wasn't enough. Now Ashley's friend had had disappeared, which compromised everything. This had been the biggest shock of all. Not once, during her conversations with Caroline had they considered this possibility, that someone other than Ashley might be taken. It was why she had agreed to let the boy stay overnight; she had been confident the boy would be safe. And now look what had happened. The poor kid's parents grief-stricken and in deep shock, nothing she could tell them to alleviate their suffering. That stupid detective hanging around, more reason to keep an eye on them. Everything that could go wrong was going wrong.

With the kids back at school and Keith at work, Rebecca arrived at Bradwell Cemetery and hesitated before entering. It was busier than usual today, relatives and loved ones perhaps checking to see if there had been more desecrations. She spotted two police officers casually hanging around, no doubt hoping to catch some weird-looking creep lurking in the area.

The priest was also wandering about the grounds, and this made her more nervous than anything else. He had nearly caught her last time. There she was screaming at Keith for being so stupid and it had been her who had only managed to escape when she fortuitously glanced behind her and saw the vicar coming. Had he recognised her? She guessed not, although should he happen to look her way now there was always the possibility. She had been reckless in trying to protect her family and no one would be thanking her if she was caught digging up someone's grave.

She waited until the vicar crossed to the other side of the grounds then moved in the opposite direction towards her mother's grave. Things were moving along too fast and needed slowing down. She still wasn't ready yet and Ashley's birthday was in just a few days. The culmination of years of preparation were coming to a head and it was all on her. She would rather kill herself than let anything happen to her son.

Rebecca arrived at her mother's grave and grimaced. The vicar and the groundskeeper must have noticed the state of the surrounding area, but no attempt had been made at cleaning the woman's headstone which now looked a hundred years old and was covered in bird droppings. The grass was brown as if there had been a fire recently, and the plants in the immediate vicinity looked like they'd been there for centuries. The graves next to hers were in pristine condition.

She knelt down, careful not to enter the circle of death and stared for a while at the mound where her mother lay directly below. Someone had filled the soil back in again, so the groundsman and vicar must be aware of the conditions surrounding the grave. This made her wonder why the vicar hadn't contacted her. It was abnormal.

She imagined Keith here with his shovel, trying to dig her up, no doubt sweating profusely, cursing the old woman and looking out for the police.

"How did you do it, Mother? How did you take that boy? It should have been impossible, so how did you do it? And where is he? Down there with you, keeping you company, you spiteful, nasty old bitch?"

She waited for a reply that wouldn't come. Not here. Back at the house she might have answered. That was where she retained her power—the place where she had died, not where she currently resided. Rebecca wasn't entirely sure how the whole process worked, only that in doing what she had before dying, in summoning those things, her spirit retained some kind of physical presence during the transformation. The change that would take place on Ashley's thirteenth birthday, when her firstborn became a teenager. The moment Edna had been waiting for all these years.

"I'm not going to let you. You know that, don't you? You should have just let go when you killed dad, carried on with your life and focused on raising me. You had everything—money, a mansion, the whole place to yourself. You could have found someone else, even, but grief and rage got the better of you. You should have just sold the mansion and moved. That place was too big for just the two of us, but you lost that as well, until you had nothing. Because even I wasn't good enough for you anymore. You ruined everything. You were no better than dad. And you're not going to ruin it for my family, too."

She pulled out the small bag from her purse and opened it. Again, careful not to enter the dead zone, she circled the grave pouring salt while mumbling a short prayer. Suddenly, she spun around, thinking someone was watching. A sinister cackling reverberated around the grounds, that might have been a murder of crows flying overhead. It was coming from nearby, yet nobody was in the vicinity. The chuckling came again and that was when she realised it was coming from within.

"Laugh all you like, Mother," she whispered, determined not to give her the satisfaction of seeing her scared. "I could come back tonight and dig up your grave like I did the others. I wouldn't be caught. They think it was Keith. They think they've caught the person desecrating the graves. Leave us alone or I will, and you'll remain down there forever."

She hoped that was the case, anyway. She still needed one more heart to complete the process. Her plan had been to do it last night, but the disappearance of Ashley's friend had ruined that idea. She still had three more days until Ashley's birthday, plenty of time. She hoped.

"*It's too late*," came a voice in her head. "It was always too late. You can't stop me now. I have the boy's soul with me. Soon I will have the real soul I need to return. Such a sweet boy."

"You bitch. I should have killed you when I had the chance. Stop this before it gets out of hand. but it doesn't matter now, I'll be ready and waiting for you. You can't leave your grave now. I've put salt all around. You know that as well as I do."

"Who said I need to leave my grave? This is just a resting place while I grow stronger. I could take Ashley's soul right now if I so wished. But I'm patient. I've been patient all these years, watching him grow. Soon, Rebecca, so very soon."

The chuckling returned, rattling her bones, causing a headache. And the worst thing was that she knew her mother was right. If she so wanted, she could take Ashley this very night. But then things wouldn't work out exactly as she hoped for. With three days left until the boy's birthday, Rebecca had one final risk to take; come back here at night and retrieve the final heart she needed to stop the old woman's spirit from returning to physical form. She just hoped and prayed that stupid nosy detective wasn't keeping too close an eye on her and her family.

Chapter

21

"It's your birthday in a couple of days, but you don't look very excited about it. How's it feel to become a teenager? I can't wait," asked Karl

The two brothers sat on Karl's bed—a rare occasion, but Ashley didn't want to be alone. Anything except being alone in his room.

"It feels horrible," he replied bluntly.

Karl's eyes widened.

Ashley never swore in front of his little brother, but there was no other word for it. He wasn't even sure he was going to make it to his birthday.

"You're scared, aren't you? I can tell. To be honest, so am I. I heard some of what Mum and Dad were talking about. Is Dad really going to prison? Something about desecrating a grave, whatever that means."

"It's desecrating, not desecrating, but I don't know. I don't think so. Who knows?"

"So what's des…desecrating mean?"

"It's like…breaking into places."

"I thought I heard them talking about Grandma's grave. He was going to break into that?"

"No."

Karl might be several years younger, but he wasn't stupid. He'd picked up on the atmosphere in the house, and now that Kevin had disappeared, things were even more tense and sad. When Ashley went to school this morning, all the kids had wanted to know what happened, who kidnapped his friend. But Ashley had said nothing, on the verge of tears and wanted to be anywhere but there. Even the teachers had given him funny, suspicious looks all day. He couldn't blame them; he must have looked guilty as hell.

"Is it about your friend? Do you really not know what happened to him? How can he just disappear like that? Without anyone hearing anything? Maybe he just ran off. My friend's friend did that once, and the police found him trying to hitchhike to London."

"No, Karl. He didn't run away. He—"

"It was Grandma, wasn't it? She took him. Somehow, she's not really dead and came and took him. I've read books about that—zombies and vampires and things that come back from the dead. Is she going to come for us, too?"

What to say? His brother had a right to know what he thought was happening. There was a chance Grandma might come for him as well, although he didn't think so— She would have done so already. But, at the same time, he didn't want to scare him anymore than he already was. Besides, the kid might blab to his friends at school, and then everyone would know. They might think he'd done something to Kevin. Then that detective would find out, and Ashley himself might get arrested.

"No, she's dead, Karl. People don't come back from the dead. Monsters don't exist. Maybe Kevin did run off or something. I don't know anymore."

He felt terrible for saying it, lying like that, but he had no choice. He'd heard his parents talking earlier again. Apparently the detective had been back that afternoon, asking loads of questions and had said he might want to speak with Ashley again. So, if he told Karl the truth, there was also the chance he might blab to the detective as well. All he knew right now was that he didn't want to sleep alone ever again, not until something was done about Grandma.

"So, can I sleep with you tonight? I'll sleep on the floor if you like. I just don't wanna sleep in my room for a while," asked Ashley, dejected

Normally Karl would have pulled a face and said no, coming up with an excuse about Ashley snoring too loud or farting all night, but he agreed instantly. It said a lot about how scared he was too.

"Thanks."

Ashley wasn't sure if it would work or not; after all, he had asked Kevin to stay over thinking that would dissuade Grandma from trying to get to him. The last thing he had expected was for Kevin to be taken instead, so what difference would it make to sleep in Karl's room? She could creep in while they were both asleep and whisk Ashley off, and Karl would never know. Then, tomorrow, it would be him answering the detective's questions. And no matter how much he thought about it where was Kevin?

Things just didn't make any sense. Dad had gone to her grave to dig her up and yet Kevin had been taken from his room. Had she risen from her grave, come all the way over here without being seen, then taken Kevin back with her? How had she then filled the hole in again?

The other night, Grandma had tried to drag Ashley into her old bedroom, not back to the cemetery, so…maybe she had taken Kevin there. Maybe she wasn't in the cemetery at all but still hidden in her bedroom. If that was the case, had Mum or Dad been in there to check? He didn't think so. They would have found Kevin's remains, surely. *So where was he*?

The only thing that seemed certain was that his birthday was coming up, and there was a very good chance he might not live to see it. And no one was doing a thing to stop Grandma, it seemed. He had a good mind to go and dig her grave up himself, maybe burn her corpse if it was still there. But what if her body wasn't in the coffin; then what? So many questions.

The setting of the sun was like a heavy weight falling into Ashley's stomach simultaneously. As night fell and the clock ticked ominously by, he couldn't stop wondering if this would be his last night on Earth. He thought about creeping into his parents' bed later, when they were asleep. Last time he tried, his mother had been furious and kicked him out. Why weren't they doing more to protect him? Go to a hotel for a few days, take him to a relative's house for a while until they sorted this whole mess out. Hell, even Aunt Caroline's would be better than this. But for now, tonight, it was too late, anyway.

Their parents came up to kiss them goodnight. When Ashley told them he would be staying in Karl's room, both raised their eyebrows but said nothing. They lingered for a while as if wanting to say something but eventually they left. It took a long time, but Ashley finally fell asleep.

Some time later, he awoke again, unsure why, and almost screamed his head off when he saw the figure slouched on a chair next to his bed. It was only when he realised it was his father sleeping there.

Ashley grinned and fell back asleep. Some questions had been answered, it seemed.

Chapter

22

Edna's story

Rebecca was two years old now, such a bright and cheerful girl, always singing and smiling. It broke Edna's heart. Such a handful, too, as she raced along the corridors with her dolls and toy prams, demanding answers to anything and everything. It was amazing that Rebecca didn't get lost in the huge mansion as she tore about the place.

The little girl was the only one that wore a smile in the mansion these days. This wasn't so difficult a premise given that now it was just Rebecca and her mother who lived here. After the incident with Richard, it hadn't taken long for the maids and the cook to discover what had really happened. Once the police had finished their investigation, 'accidental death' being the conclusion reached, they had all resigned. Edna hadn't bothered searching for new employees. And so, the house soon began to fall into disarray.

Rebecca's joyful singing and beaming smile broke her heart because she knew it wasn't her doing, but the natural product of being a toddler, oblivious to the realities around her. Edna desperately wanted to be the best possible mother she could be, provide her with everything Alison had never had, but Edna had soon lost all will to live herself after killing Richard. Now she was alone and the weight of her responsibilities and the loneliness within the walls of this house were an overbearing load for her. Soon, darker thoughts started possessing her mind, as though that cursed Ouija board had allowed more corrupt shadows and spirits to enter her world and they were slowly poisoning her. As if the mansion itself was slowly crumbling around her, feeding her negativity as the dust and decay mounted.

After the initial investigation, Edna had been careful to appear the grief-stricken widower among Richard's friends who phoned to enquire about what had happened and the subsequent police investigation, so she wouldn't fall under suspicion. If the police or the insurance company suspected anything, she could lose the house and everything. She had nowhere to go with a young child to bring up, and this could never happen. So she shed tears, when necessary, kept a lowkey profile. But when the house was finally passed to her as was all of Richard's wealth, she felt confident enough to finally start enjoying life again. After all, this had been her intention all along—provide Rebecca with all the love and support she could ever need and never have to worry about anything else again.

   She had planned on putting Rebecca in school, have all her friends over, so they could lead that normal life again she so desired. But her strength, both of mind and body, faded with time, leaving her virtually a recluse. She became the eccentric widower, barely seen in the village, refusing to answer calls on her wellbeing. The house had declined into what some might have considered to be abandoned, had they ventured inside. That Rebecca was fed and washed each day seemed as much as Edna could do. She barely took care of herself anymore.

   As the house slowly ate her morale, and her loneliness and depression grew stronger, she started thinking about all the things Richard had done. His obsession with the afterlife, returning again ready to start afresh, learn from past mistakes. She thought of Alison, her firstborn, somewhere up there suffering intensely because Edna had failed to protect her from her father. She started seeing shadows in the house, ghostly silhouettes in every corner, usually in her peripheral vision and was convinced it was Richard, having indeed come back from the dead to torment her forever.

   Edna would wake in the middle of the night and scream at some dark form hovering above or beside her bed. Reflections in mirrors were Richard lurking just behind her, waiting for the right moment to push her down the stairs, meaning Rebecca would be taken into care. She saw Alison scurrying along the hallways, somehow in league with her father, both of them conspiring to kill her so she would spend all eternity in that dark place Alison had spoke of. Her world was one of intense paranoia and torment, and slowly but surely, words and ideas crept into her mind.

As the months passed, the house fell into even more disarray, as did her finances. Not having the business knowledge of her late husband, and ignoring desperate calls from solicitors and lawyers, she squandered money, thanks in large part to a grave recession and plummeting stock market. Soon, when holes started to appear in the roof and cracks in the plaster, the boiler that kept the whole house warm in winter failed to work. The money wasn't there anymore to repair them.

When Rebecca was five, she attended school, mainly so Edna didn't have to deal with her anymore rather than wanting to provide her with a good education. Questions were soon asked. One of the teachers heard Rebecca talk about the leaking roof and being so cold at nights, that her mother barely acknowledged her presence, so inspectors were called to the mansion. They didn't like what they saw.

By now Edna was barely aware of Rebecca's existence. She had submerged herself in the world of the afterlife and the occult, spending hour upon hour reading books on the subject. She stayed up into the late hours conversing with spirits. wanting to know what came next, whether there was choice, if Alison was out there somewhere.

When winter came, she simply wrapped herself and Rebecca in more blankets. To stop the rainwater from seeping in Edna covered the holes in the roof with cardboard. She saw it as nothing more than a distraction, taking her away from her consultations with the afterlife. Even Rebecca became an annoying distraction, left to practically fend for herself while Edna locked herself in the study and inadvertently followed in the same footsteps as Richard. Edna's world was of misery and torment, and she wanted no part of it. She wanted to leave this world, start all over again—her and her two daughters. For all of them to lead a normal life, and forget the pain of death and loss.

She learned that Richard had been right, after all; a choice could be given to her if she followed certain rites and passages, and summoned the right spirits. It would require a great deal of patience and a series of events to occur for it to happen, but it could be done. After learning this, Edna began the process that would lead to a culmination in years to come, one that would see her leave behind this world and start all over again, as things were meant to be.

And then came the final straw in the destruction of Edna's mental health. The last nail in the coffin that sealed off any semblance of empathy towards the world and those around her that had died during the years alone at the crumbling mansion. When Rebecca was eight years old, the authorities had decided Edna was not fit to be a mother anymore. They took her daughter from her and placed her in a foster home. The choice was simple; recover from the depression and mental illness that had invaded her body or she wouldn't see her daughter again until she was eighteen and could choose herself.

Shortly afterwards, Edna finally sold the mansion for a pittance and moved into a small apartment some miles away. She next saw Rebecca on her eighteenth birthday, when the young woman was released from care and decided to make a visit. But Edna's mind was too far gone to care anymore.

Chapter

23

When Keith told her he was going to be staying in Ash's room at night to ensure the same didn't happen to their son as Kevin, Rebecca agreed it was a good idea. She would have done the same herself, but it would have raised questions she wasn't ready to answer yet. Not yet. Not quite. All in good time. She knew perfectly well where Kevin was, but she couldn't explain things to her poor, terrified husband until it was all over. Then she would tell him, although, admittedly, she had an idea that Keith had pretty much guessed what was happening, anyway. And he wasn't too wrong. If she could keep him from doing anything stupid until the time arrived, it would be enough. Besides, he had been accused of desecrating a grave and a boy had gone missing from their home as well which meant he had to keep a low profile. At least until the court case was over. Then, hopefully, he would receive a simple fine.

It also meant that with Keith sleeping in their son's bedroom with both boys, she could continue with her own plans without disturbing him or alerting his suspicions. It was risky—very risky—but she had no choice. Her only hope was that the detective believed he already had the culprit and had told the police force they didn't need to check the cemetery on such a regular basis anymore. The back side to this was that he might have someone keeping a regular check on her home instead. But it was too late for that now—the risk would have to be taken. A cat or dog was always an option in case of emergencies, but there was no way she would kill an animal to fulfil her part of the deal

Constantly checking behind her to see if she was being followed, she made it to the cemetery and climbed over the gate, glad that she had decided to start hitting the gym shortly after Karl was born. Not just to lose weight but also because she had an idea back then she might end up doing something like this one day and wanted to be prepared. Keith had told her in private that trying to dig up the old bitch's coffin had nearly killed him, once her anger had died down. She had laughed, but knew the feeling well. Too well.

Rebecca grabbed the shovel she'd brought with her and headed straight towards the grave that had recently been filled in. With a good supply of bottled water and some high energy chocolate bars in her rucksack to provide her with much needed strength, she had another quick look around, then started digging.

She had seen the obituary in that morning's paper and made the decision there and then. She should have started this much sooner—Ashley's birthday was in a couple of days and time was up. She was extremely lucky some poor unfortunate sod had died recently, giving her a fresh opportunity.

She wasn't exactly thrilled at the prospect of using a human heart, either. But when she and Caroline had discussed Edna's growing descent into madness, she had known even then that she was definitely going through with their plan. Again, like now, she had been left no choice. It was either her or Caroline, and her friend would have died of a heart attack had she attempted this mad and grotesque plan. But it was the only way to stop Edna. Even if the woman died— accidently or not—she had already done enough damage that in time nothing would stop her. All they could do—all Rebecca could do—was try and counteract the invocation through the morbid and disgusting way.

"I should have just choked the old witch," she muttered as she dug deeper and deeper.

She hated herself for not doing something sooner and hated Caroline for refusing to cooperate in this seemingly mad plan of hers, because God would send her to Hell for blasphemy. She couldn't even tell Keith about it when Edna had been reciting those passages, doing the exact same thing Rebecca was doing right now under his nose. Keith was too naïve, not believing in these things. He just thought his mother-in-law had been turning senile and spiteful in her old age, messing about with black magic, that it was just superstition.

Hadn't he seen how she had been kicked out of church for desecration herself? Hadn't he heard her rambling, seemingly incoherent rantings at night when she was locked away in her bedroom? It seemed like the whole neighbourhood could have heard her chanting. Many a time, Rebecca had burst into her room, screaming at her to stop. Tussles had ensued, but Edna had refused to listen, laughing in her daughter's face. Edna had succumbed to madness and a morbid fascination with the afterlife, and no amount of pleading or threatening would have changed that.

Eventually, the shovel connected with something solid. She stood up, stretched her back, and rested for a second before finishing what she had come for. A bottle of water was finished in barely two swigs and a chocolate bar consumed. It was quite a cold night, but her back was soaked with sweat and her muscles screamed in protest. She kept telling herself this was the last one; after this, the worst was over. Almost the worst, anyway.

Once she had her breath back, she scraped away the last of the soil. She peered out from the hole to make sure she was alone, then forced open the coffin lid with a crowbar she'd brought with her. As always, she grimaced at the sight of the dead woman looking back up at her and was glad the corpse seemed to have died of natural causes. A nasty road accident, for example, would have given her yet more nightmares to contend with. Not wanting to push her luck any longer, she pulled out the machete she kept hidden from her husband and deftly began to open up the woman's chest, hacking at it in her desperation to get the job done so she could get out of there. Eventually, she could fit both hands into the woman's chest cavity and cut out the corpse's heart. She sealed it in a plastic bag, put it back in her rucksack, and climbed out.

"Sorry, ma'am," she muttered, and ran from the cemetery.

Arriving back home, she tried to keep as quiet as possible, praying neither her husband or the kids awoke needing the toilet. She unlocked her dead mother's room, closing the door gently behind her. Tucked away in the wardrobe, in a locked box, was a book—an ancient one Caroline had acquired many years ago. It was probably extremely valuable by now, but its practical value was much higher.

For Rebecca, this was the worst part. Much more so than the risk of being caught desecrating a grave. She brought out the heart and her trusty pocket knife, and while reciting certain passages from the book, chopped the raw heart into small enough pieces that she didn't have to chew. Then, she ate it.

This time she only gagged five times before putting everything away again. After leaving the room, she had a quick shower, then climbed into bed, feeling exhausted. Finally, she was ready to face her mother.

Chapter

24

Keith could take no more. He'd been trying to be funny around the kids, asking Ash what he would like for his birthday. A Barbie, perhaps. Some Lego figures, which normally would have provoked huge laughs and merciless teasing from Karl. A red-faced Ashley would have looked sheepish and embarrassed in the corner. But he barely got a shrug from Ash, not even a smirk from Karl. It might have been someone else's birthday they were celebrating—some cousin they hadn't seen in years. It was enough for Keith to know that both his kids were terrified of whatever lurked in that bedroom. Of the same happening to them that had Kevin.

It had to stop.

Keith wasn't much in the mood for celebrating birthdays, either. But he had to make an effort, try and evoke a little normality in their lives somehow without all the doom and gloom currently swallowing them up. It was as if everyone was on the verge of bursting into tears. Or having a heart attack at the slightest groan or creak given up by the house. Kevin disappearing from their home was the absolute last thing he had expected. He had his suspicions about what had happened, but he could barely bring himself to believe them. It was the twenty-first century, for God's sake. This superstitious crap was believed in during the medieval times, not now. But that wasn't going to bring the boy back, was it?

If someone didn't do something to stop all this, and soon, Keith had a pretty good idea Kevin might not be the only one disappearing. It was why he had decided to start sleeping in their room, to keep an eye on things. Ash had apparently had a similar thought—safety in numbers. Hadn't worked for Kevin, though. His two sons were up there now, practically inseparable. They had never been typical brothers that fought all the time, arguing over stupid things but they had never been particularly close either. Both he and Rebecca had assumed it was the age difference, each with their own set of friends and their own devices. But these last few days, they were like twins. It melted Keith's heart, and he could see the same in Rebecca's eyes—the same sense of immense sadness and helplessness that coursed through him. But if Rebecca was going to be so stubborn about her mother, it was all on him. And the time had finally come.

"So, Rebecca?" asked Keith.

"Huh?" she muttered, sitting next to him on the sofa.

"After everything that has happened and all that we spoke about, are you going to fix this or what? And don't play ignorant with me; you know what I'm talking about."

Rebecca's shoulders sagged. She refused to meet Keith's eyes, staring straight at the TV. He could tell from the way she chewed on her lower lip that she was debating with herself internally. "I'm fixing it, Keith. I promise. Just…I'm not ignoring things—far from it—but you gotta let things run their course."

"*Run their course*?! Rebecca, in case you hadn't noticed, a kid went missing from our home! We've got the police watching us, probably wondering if we're kid killers or something. Must think we're part of some satanic cult after catching me digging up your mother's grave! But you're fixing it? Well, would you mind speeding up a bit?"

"I know how it sounds, Keith. And yes, I am aware that a kid went missing. And yes, after *you* got caught acting like a ghoul in the graveyard, yeah, we're probably under surveillance."

"After what you said the other day, I've been wondering if I'm not the only ghoul in this household."

"Don't talk nonsense. Just…bear with me okay. She was my mother. I know how to stop all this crap from continuing."

"But what is this crap? Why won't you tell me what's going on? Even if I and the kids are beginning to get an idea of what that is."

"Keith, you wouldn't believe me if I told you. When it's all over—and I promise it soon will be—I'll explain everything."

"Well, it's not good enough. Your children are terrified, sleeping together in the same bed. They didn't even do that when they were younger. And we have a child who has disappeared from our home, whose parents must be horrified and nearly suicidal with grief. I've been thinking…"

He let the words float there, like a hangman's noose, dangling before her eyes. It worked, because she finally turned to face him, eyebrows raised. "I'm taking the kids to my mothers. Until you *fix* this."

"*What*? No way, uh-huh. You're not taking my kids anywhere. You leave them alone. They'll be perfectly fine. Trust me."

"Trust you? Are you hearing yourself? How long before Ash or Karl disappears like Ash's friend? No way, Rebecca, I'm sorry, but I can't risk anything happening to them. You do what you have to, and when it's fixed, I'll bring them back."

"No way, Keith. You take my kids, I'll call the poli—"

They both tilted their heads towards the ceiling when a loud thud sounded directly above them. It had come from Rebecca's mother's room.

"What was that?" asked Keith. "Was that one of the kids just falling out of bed?"

The lightbulb above their heads swayed back and forth. Keith was sure he could hear a rumble, as if thunder was heading their way. There came a loud scraping as if something heavy was being dragged along the floor.

"Oh no," muttered Keith, and dashed towards the stairs.

Rebecca was right behind him. They both burst into Karl's room, and Rebecca was about to flick the light switch, when Keith stopped her.

"No, don't," he whispered, and pointed to the bed. Both kids were fast asleep in bed, snoring gently.

Quietly, they left the room and closed the door. From behind them came something resembling a snort or groan. Another thud came, something falling against the wall. Grandma's wall.

Ignoring Rebecca, Keith headed straight to his mother-in-law's old room and tried the door. As always, it was locked. He barged it with his shoulder, achieving nothing.

"Keith!" hissed Rebecca. "Stop!"

"Open the door, Rebecca, or I'll kick it down. You heard it as well as I did. What or who is in there?"

"Nothing is in there, only her old furniture. You are not kicking that door down."

"No? Watch me." He took a step back and raised his right leg.

"Keith, stop it! You'll wake the kids. Don't be stupid."

"I'm not. I'm doing what I should have done a long time ago. Now stand back."

"Okay, wait!"

She went straight to their bedroom and came back with the key. Another thud came from within, then what might have been a growl, followed by a wheezed groan. Rebecca made to unlock the door but hesitated, long enough for Keith to lose his patience. He snatched the key from her, unlocked the door, then threw it open. Instinctively, he tried to turn on the light, but the bulb exploded, glass flying everywhere. He stormed in regardless.

The moment he did, he was instantly reminded of what happened to him before the dreaded wardrobe. But this time he was determined not to be afraid anymore—his kids depended on him. His phone in his pocket, he grabbed it and turned on the light app, waving the strong beam around the room.

It was empty.

He threw open the wardrobe doors, his heart heavy in his throat, expecting for Edna to reach for him with outstretched, rotting arms. But this didn't happen either.

He almost screamed when Rebecca touched his arm.

"See?" she hissed. "I told you there is no one in here."

But her eyes told a different story.

Chapter

25

Ashley mumbled incoherencies and absently rubbed his eyes. He'd been having a weird dream again, although, thankfully, nothing too horrific or scary. Not that he could recall, anyway. But there had been banging and hissing and shouting that might have been his parents. He wasn't sure. It sounded like them, and he was pretty sure his grandma was involved again. That didn't surprise him at all. It was all he could think about. That and his bladder, which was screaming at him for release. He really did not want to go out there in the pitch black. He'd asked if a light could be left on in the hallway, but Mum told him they couldn't afford to waste electric and he needed to grow up. That stung.

Beside him, Karl was snoring heavier than usual, as if he had a cold or sore throat or something. That was the last thing he needed—to get ill. He was already not feeling well as it was—in his mind, at least. Sleeping right next to a gestating snot monster was not cool at all. And now that he thought about it,

Karl must have been really sweating and tossing and turning all night. Ashley was right on the edge of the bed, and Karl stank of sweat.

"Hey, Karl. Move over, will ya?" He pushed him.

Karl groaned in protest and pulled the blankets up covering his nostrils. Good. At least this way he didn't have to smell him. Tomorrow, he was going to give him hell about that. If his brother was developing some nasty illness, he could sleep on the sofa. Shoving Karl had temporarily taken his mind off his bladder, but now it was back, and with a vengeance. Experience told him it wasn't going to go away until he relieved the problem.

He jumped out of bed and dashed to the toilet, all while praying that his grandma's bedroom door didn't suddenly fly open. That his grandmother didn't attempt to snatch him up. He made it back to bed without the slightest sound or movement coming from anywhere.

When he went to jump back into bed, Karl had once again sprawled out across the bed, almost hogging the whole thing for himself. With both hands, Ashley pushed him back to his side of the bed. His hands came away soaking wet which nearly made Ashley gag. Disgusted, he wiped them on Karl's pillow. For good measure, Ashley took as much of the blanket as he could, covering his nose again. Unfortunately, this allowed the wave of eye-watering sweat to drift up to his nostrils, regardless and he almost gagged. This kid had a fever, it seemed, his breath coming in wheezed, harsh gasps, almost like panting. It made Ashley worry for him.

"Hey, Karl. You okay, man?"

Karl snorted in response and choked back what sounded like a huge ball of phlegm. "Leave me alone," he grunted.

Christ, it didn't even sound like Karl. It was as if he had the nastiest, biggest cold and his chest was made entirely of snot and mucus. There had to be a lake of the stuff swimming about in there. And he smelled really bad.

Ashley thought about going downstairs to sleep on the sofa. Maybe he should go and wake his mum and tell her. The kid might be really ill.

Karl turned over and slapped an arm on Ashley's chest, as though cuddling him. It was like being punched, taking the wind from him. His arm and hand were clammy and soaked with sweat as it rubbed across his bare chest. Karl's face was mere inches from his own. His breath smelled as if he'd been eating rotting vegetables for a week and hadn't brushed his teeth in just as long. The stench came in waves as his mouth opened to inhale and exhale loudly. The heat coming off of his brother made Ashley sweat as well. This was some fever, and it was practically impossible that Ashley wouldn't get infected with it.

"Karl, man, get off!" he hissed. "You stink, man. Get away from me."

"Leave me alone. Give me a kiss."

Ashley froze. What did he just say? What kind of dream was he having?

Karl leaned over and kissed Ashley on the cheek—a big, smoochy kiss like his grandmother used to give him, lips fat and wet, lingering for far too long.

"What the Hell, Karl! Get off!"

He pushed him away, but it was as if Karl had grown three times the size in the last five minutes. Ashley couldn't budge the kid.

"Such a sweet little boy," Karl said again in the husky voice. "Give me a kiss. Soon we'll be together again."

Then he felt his brother's tongue run over his cheek, followed by another sloppy kiss.

That freaked Ashley enough that he jumped out of bed. He dashed over to the light switch and flicked it on. Then he screamed.

A huge lump sat in Karl's bed staring back at him. The bed sagged in the middle, such was the weight—a great dead thing with grey skin peeling from her body, muscle tissue showing through the holes where her flesh used to be. Her lips, only seconds before having been planted on his cheek, dangled from her face as she tried and failed to grin at him. When she puckered them to imitate another kiss, they fell off.

"Come to Grandma, baby. Give me a kiss," she wheezed, holding out flabby arms, the flesh barely hanging on beneath.

Ashley turned and bolted.

And yet, once he was outside on the landing, there she was again, her arms reaching for him, great bulk swaying back and forth in front of her bedroom door. Two hands grabbed him around the neck and started dragging him towards her. He punched and swung at her, yet his fists went straight through her, punching thin air. Somehow, frantically struggling and writhing, he managed to break free from her grasp and burst into his parent's room.

"Mum! Dad! It's Grandma! She got me. Help!"

Dad must have forgotten his promise to sleep in their room because he bolted upright alongside Mum, and both stared at him groggily for a moment until his words caused the desired effect. Both jumped out of bed and dashed towards him.

"Are you okay? What are you talking about?" babbled his mother.

"It's Grandma! I was in bed, and I thought Karl had a fever or something. When I came back from the toilet, it wasn't him, though. It was Grandma lying there. Then I ran out here and there she was outside her bedroom. And she tried to drag me in!"

Keith made to run to the room, but Rebecca stuck out an arm and held him back. "No! Stay here. Let me check."

She practically barged past Ashley and stormed out of the room. Keith remained where he was, face red, eyes bulging. Ashley followed his mother and saw her standing tentatively at the door to Grandma's room. Then she stepped in, muttering something under her breath. He could barely hear or understand what she was saying until he was right behind her.

"Be gone; I command thee. Return to your grave; I command thee. You are not welcome here, now or ever. Leave; I command thee." She repeated the mantra several times over and over then stopped; her head cocked as if listening for a reply. But nothing came.

When she turned around, she almost tripped over her feet when she saw Ashley standing there. "I told you to wait outside! Why don't you listen?!" she hissed.

Ashley was shocked, hearing her swear at him. And what had she been muttering? Was it a spell or curse or something? He had been right, after all; Grandma was a vampire or some sort of monster, and she wanted him.

"It's true! You knew all along. Grandma wants to bite me and eat me and you *knew*! And you did nothing! And she's gonna do it on my birthday. She told me!"

"Ashley, stop," she said gently. "No one's a vampire. No one is coming for you. You're perfectly safe. I swear. Nothing is going to happen to you. I promise. Go back to bed."

Keith joined them outside Grandma's room. He looked at them both, but glared at his wife who said nothing and locked the door again.

"Back to bed. Everyone," said Rebecca

Ashley hesitantly entered Karl's room, checking to make sure it was Karl in there. His brother was fast asleep oblivious to everything. There was no sign of Grandma having been there.

Ashley cried himself to sleep on the floor for the rest of the night.

Chapter

26

Edna's story

It may have been the fact that Rebecca was pregnant for the first time that changed her attitude towards Edna. Impending motherhood had a habit of doing that, Edna had come to learn—a sense of overwhelming guilt of all the bad things a person did to their parents and what was surely to happen to them as well. The reminiscing.

'Remember when I did this and that?'

'Remember the day you grounded me because…'

'What a naughty girl I was, I'm so sorry to have put you through all that. You're the best Mum ever…'

This case was slightly different, though. Rebecca had been taken from her when she was eight years old and, while she said she could barely remember much before that, she did know that Edna had pretty much left her to her own devices while Edna's sanity crumbled around her. On Rebecca's eighteenth birthday, curiosity had got the better of her. She had wanted to see her mother, find out what had gone wrong. But Edna was in no position to reminisce and rekindle those terrible moments that had led up to her current state of mind. On the advice of the very few family members willing enough to speak with her, it had been recommended that she spend a short time in Northgate, try and get her thoughts back together. Rebecca would be waiting for her in a few years, and she owed this to her only living daughter.

But it had been a complete waste of time. No matter what drugs they gave her, the group and single therapy sessions, only one thing remained on Edna's mind. And it refused to budge.

Starting over again.

Literally.

She barely even recognised Rebecca when she came to see her, now a fully-grown woman, much less remembered her name. At first, she had called her Alison. It had taken considerable effort on Rebecca's part to convince her Alison was dead. The last few years of Edna's life were a complete blur. After leaving Northgate, she returned home to her beloved Ouija board and her spirit friends, who by now had taught her enough— along with the help of several obscure library books she had managed to obtain—to carry out her plans. Everything was ready. Almost ready, she soon learned. And then Rebecca showed up.

Edna's living conditions and her own personal hygiene must have been a little worse than what she expected, though. When Rebecca knocked on her door, her eyes had widened like saucers, and she had wrinkled her nose. Admittedly, she couldn't remember the last time she had had a shower or a haircut or even depilated her legs. She guessed she resembled a man in many ways, as Rebecca pointed out. So, after the initial shock, they had chatted—or rather, Rebecca had submitted her to a barrage of questions. They didn't see each other again until a few years later.

Twice, Edna had tried to pass over to the other side. On both occasions, it had failed dramatically, to the point she had been hospitalised for attempted suicide. Then she was sent back to Northgate indefinitely. There was something seriously missing in Edna's plans, and it wasn't until the next time she saw her daughter that she learned what the problem was.

Rebecca was pregnant.

To Edna, Rebecca was nothing more than a lost memory, a ghost haunting her past. But her being pregnant changed everything. The last piece in a chain of puzzles was now complete…almost.

This time, when Rebecca walked into her festering, filthy home, it wasn't to tell her mother to get her act together, pull herself together, and stop reminiscing over the past, but something totally unexpected.

"I've been thinking, Mum. Now that I'm pregnant, it's changed something in me, the way I see things. I'm ready to forget the past, what little of it I can remember, anyway. And seeing you like this, a hermit, cooped up in this place, with all those terrible memories eating away at you…Well, I was talking to Keith, my husband, and basically, we'd like you to move in with us. Where I can keep an eye on you. Get you cleaned up. Actually, we should probably do that first, before you meet my husband! What do you think?"

Edna thought this was a very good idea. There might have been a smile on her face as she considered her options, something that barely crossed her lips in years. She didn't want to sound too eager, though, make her daughter suspicious in any way. So she said she would think about it. "I don't want to scare your husband and the baby!" she said jokingly. Yet, this was the last thing she cared about. Finally, after nearly twenty years of planning and practising, she thought she could finally do what Richard had obsessed and failed over for so long.

"Hi, umm, Edna, nice to finally meet you. I've heard so much about you," said Keith the day she moved in.

Edna didn't need to be psychic or require the help of her spirit friends to know her son-in-law was lying. She could see it in his eyes, the way he forced the smile to appear. Rebecca had done a wonderful job of completely changing Edna's aspect; taking her to get her hair cut, so now it was short and grey, tightly rolled into a bun. She personally dragged her mother into the bathtub and shaved her legs, the moustache above her lip and hairs on her chin. She went and bought new clothes, which must have been tougher than expected. Edna had more than doubled her weight since Rebecca was taken from her—but none of this changed what was hidden within. Her mind was still as dark and festering as that fateful day. But she had to make an effort, try and appear normal and be excited for her future grandson, make a fuss of her daughter. At first, she managed it. But her energy levels were soon depleted and, more often than not, she preferred to lock herself away in her new bedroom and study and practice with her secret books.

"There's something wrong about her. She gives me the creeps," she often heard Keith saying in the adjacent bedroom at night. "There's something in her eyes, gives me Charles Manson vibes. And I hear her talking to herself a lot, but I swear it's not in any language I've heard before."

"Give her time, Keith. She lived alone for so long that she's struggling to fit in. She went through a lot."

That was an understatement. Edna smiled to herself as she listened to them talking about her. If only they knew…

When Ashley was born, it was like a fire was lit in Edna's heart. Her daughter and son-in-law assumed the huge, beaming smile on her face was for being proud at finally becoming a grandmother. It was a role she took on with expert hands, using her pension to buy him toys and clothes, happily going for walks around the park while tickling his cheeks as he lay in his pram. Except for her bizarre and disturbing antics when alone in her room—according to Keith—she might have been the perfect grandmother. But still things were not ready.

Not only did Edna converse with spirits during her sessions with the Ouija board; there was also a dark, malignant entity that sometimes came to her when requested. One that Edna had specifically sought to question. It was an entity who refused to move on, finding delight in discomfort and remorse, its soul a dead, black thing and who thrived on giving its knowledge to any who deliberately sought to use it for their own personal gain.

"Tell me," she asked of it one night, "is it ready? Can I fulfil my dream after all these years of waiting?"

No, spelled out the planchette. *First you must be patient. Await a special day. Only then can you be guaranteed what you desire.*

And so, dejected, Edna had no choice but to wait.

"Oh, you are growing up to be such a special boy," she told Ashley on his fifth birthday. "One day, I will have such a surprise for you. I can hardly wait."

"When, Grandma? Can I have it now? I love surprises!"

"All in good time, my dear boy. All in good time. Now give your grandma a nice, big hug."

And, of course, he did.

On his eleventh birthday, she began the process.

Rebecca wasn't as happy though when she discovered what Edna had been doing at the local cemetery, desecrating graves.

"Are you completely mad?" screamed Rebecca. "What the hell were you thinking? It's sick! Disgusting. You're going to prison and, to be honest, I don't care. I should never have invited you to come live with us. You're as sick now as you were back then!"

To an extent, Edna could empathise. To an outsider, it probably was morbid and sick. But she had her needs and couldn't tell her daughter that. Fortunately, though, getting caught wasn't as bad or disastrous as it might have been. This time it had been more about pleasure than for any necessity. She'd already used the ones she needed but enjoyed the process so much she wanted to continue. Just in case.

"I…I thought it was Alison. I just wanted to see her one more time," she lied.

"Rubbish, Mother! This is the fourth time in the last year this has happened. How did you even manage it? You need to go back to Northgate. Permanently. If not, you're going to prison. Christ, I can't believe you've been doing this right under our noses. What are the neighbours going to think? Your grandchildren? I feel sick!"

"No one will find out. I've spoken to the police already. They understand."

"They understand that an elderly lady has been desecrating graves for the last year and stealing their organs? Namely their hearts? And what did you do with them?"

She ate them but she wasn't going to tell her that—it was all part of the process.

"I thought it was Alison's body each time. I wanted to keep a piece of her with me all the time, but…but I kept losing them, so I had to return. The police were sympathetic. They promised they'll keep it lowkey."

But some did find out. Namely Reverend Nichols who privately told her never to return to his church ever again. That was fine with her. She had no intentions of going back anyway. God was the last person who would help her.

"I want you to go to Northgate, Mum. I don't want you in my house anymore. Especially with the children around."

"I'll think about it," she said, and that was the end of that. Until the next argument.

And it came not too long afterwards. Edna already had her suspicions that Rebecca was catching on to what she was planning, because on the very rare occasions Edna left the house, things were always rearranged differently in her room when she returned. Specifically in her wardrobe and the secret compartments there. Subtle differences but differences all the same. The books she used to study were always in a different order to how she had left them. Bookmarks had been left on different pages. And the titles of these particular books could leave no doubts as to what they were about.

The following one came about when she was practising her invocations and was convinced there were eyes watching her. And not the eyes she wanted. When she threw the bedroom door open, Rebecca almost fell into the room.

"What are you doing?" asked Edna.

"And what the hell are you doing? I heard you. What was that?"

"None of your business, that's what."

"You're a witch. A horrible old witch! Get out of my house right now."

"You're going to kick your poor old mother out of your home? Leave her destitute on the streets? What will people say? What will the neighbours say when they see me wandering the streets begging for a few pennies? Or your children at school when the other kids find out? Is that what you want? I'm not hurting anyone. You let me be!" And with that, she slammed the door closed again.

It was the last time Edna spoke to her daughter—and pretty much her son-in-law, who knew something was wrong but not what.

Just a few days before she died, she cuddled up to Ashley several weeks before his thirteenth birthday. "Soon, Ashley, very soon. Remember I told you I had a surprise for you when you were older? It's almost time. On your thirteenth birthday, in fact!"

Chapter

27

If anyone had ever told him he would be dreading the day his thirteenth birthday arrived, he would have laughed in their faces. Told them they were stupid. Becoming thirteen was a milestone. The one birthday all kids looked forward to. The day they could finally call themselves a teenager. One step away from becoming an adult.

Conversely, becoming an adult seemed to have its pros and cons, because while most adults he knew seemed to lead pretty boring lives and had to work each day, it also had its benefits. Going to work meant not having to go to school, no homework, having loads of money, being able to do what one wanted without asking permission, drive a car—these were exciting things. After reaching the grand age of thirteen, the next step was eighteen, just five short years.

Now, he would do anything to go back in time, to when he had just been born. Because today he had finally reached that milestone. All he wanted to was curl up in bed and never wake up.

To make things worse, it was a Saturday, which usually would have been a good thing. But today, being at school would have helped take his mind of things. Instead, he had all day to sit and contemplate the possibilities, what may or may not happen—if he truly had imagined everything or not. If Grandma's promise was going to come true—whatever that may be.

If this wasn't bad enough, he knew from overhearing his mother on the phone that aunts and uncles would be coming over for a surprise birthday party. That was the last thing he wanted right now. To the point he was quietly sobbing as he sat on the edge of Karl's bed alone, terrified for his life. There was no way he could deal with aunts and uncles and cousins today. Not today.

The feeling seemed to be general in the household too. Normally, Karl would have combined torment with good wishes at his brother's birthday celebrations, but he was already downstairs. Normally, he would have woken Ashley early on his birthday while he still lay half asleep in bed to give him a present, which would have been some joke thing—a Barbie doll, perhaps—before the real ones later. Today, nothing.

His parents hadn't bothered poking a head in to see him either; a hug from his mother, slap on the back from Dad—nothing. Right now, Ashley didn't even want to go downstairs. He had a pretty good idea they had bought him the PlayStation 5 for his birthday, but this instilled zero enthusiasm in him. But he needed to go down. Somehow, he had to stop his relatives from coming over, tell them he was ill or something—which wasn't too far from the truth.

Begrudgingly, he rose and headed towards downstairs. He found his mother alone in the living room and sat beside her.

"Hey, happy birthday!" she said, and hugged him then kissed him on the cheek, which normally would have made him blush and pull away. This time, he did neither.

"Thanks."

"What's wrong? You don't look very happy to have finally become a teenager."

"You know what's wrong, Mum. Don't pretend you don't. I can see it on everyone's faces. I know what's going on, Dad getting caught digging up Grandma's grave, the things I've seen and heard. The things you've both been arguing about lately. Grandma's alive, isn't she? And she's coming for me; I know it. Just before she died, she said I would be getting a big surprise on my thirteenth birthday, and I think you know what that is." He was sobbing again now, staring absently at the floor.

"Ash, listen. I know there have been some weird things going on lately, and I haven't been ignoring you or it at all. It's…it's just very hard to explain, that's all, but I promise nothing is going to happen. Grandma is dead, and that's how she is going to remain. I'm going to fix a few things and everything will be back to normal again. You'll see. Today is your birthday and nothing is going to ruin it."

"That's the other thing. I'm really not in the mood for being surrounded by loads of relatives. I just want today to be over so I know for sure what Grandma said isn't true. Can't you tell them I'm ill or something? And to come over tomorrow?"

Rebecca stared at Ashley for a while, saying nothing, showing no emotion or expression. Finally, she sighed. "Okay, yeah. To be honest, I don't think anyone is in the mood for parties, what with your friend disappearing as well. I'll phone them all and tell them to come tomorrow. They'll understand."

"Thanks, Mum!"

That made him feel so much better. Yet, at the same time, the mention of Kevin almost caused his heart to crack down the centre again. He missed his friend so badly and couldn't imagine what his parents must be feeling with each new day and no news. Ashley didn't think they would ever be getting any news either. If his body at least turned up somewhere so he didn't have to guess what inexplicable things had happened to him, it might make things easier. Had he suffered? Was the same going to happen to him tonight?

Just then Karl walked into the living room and summed up completely the mood in the household, as if the air was contaminated with some despair-inducing toxin. "Hey, Ash. Happy birthday," he mumbled, and headed back up to his room.

Keith saw Ashley trudge off upstairs and wanted to run and hug him as if he hadn't seen him in months. He wanted to tell him not to worry, that everything was going to turn out fine. He wanted to grab his car keys, grab both his kids, and take them to his mother's until Rebecca sorted all this mess out. But he couldn't bring himself to do any of that. He trusted his wife more than he trusted anyone and kept telling himself that she had everything under control and would put a stop to this madness. Whatever it was that old bitch had done, she would fix it. If things went bad, he'd burn the godforsaken house down if necessary. Forget the detective and whether he was doing surveillance on them or not. They could take him to prison for arson or trying to dig up an old witch's grave, but no one was going to take his kids.

And yet, despite this show of defiance, telling himself that he would be the one to stop it all, if necessary, here he was pottering around, doing nothing in the garden. Anything to avoid being in the house and its atmosphere that hung like a poison. It killed him, being like this on his son's birthday—the big one—but he could tell from the kid's demeanor that he was as interested in presents and parties as everyone else. Even Karl had been subdued at the breakfast table. In his bedroom wardrobe sat the new PlayStation that Ash had practically got on his hands and knees and begged for when it was released. Keith and Rebecca had been so excited when they finally bought it for him, as if it was for them rather than Ashley. Now he wondered if it would sit there forever, unused.

He squatted and started pulling weeds that had barely pushed through the soil. Flashbacks of shovelling soil from Edna's grave rushed through his head, the shock of the cop catching him, hearing Rebecca insinuate it had been her that desecrated the others. God, he hoped she knew what she was doing. He froze momentarily when he thought he heard shouting coming from inside the house, then continued when he realised it was Karl laughing timidly. A dog barked next door, almost causing him to scream. He turned and looked up at the bedroom window and gasped. Someone was hiding behind a curtain watching him, and it sure as hell wasn't his wife or kids. He'd just seen them all together downstairs.

The frustration and impotence he had been feeling seconds earlier returned, causing a rage to flood his veins. Keith jumped and dashed towards the stairs. That son of a bitch woman was not going to scare him anymore. This was it. It was over.

"Where are you, you old witch?" he yelled as he burst into Ashley's bedroom.

He stopped when he saw Ashley standing there looking like he'd just been caught doing something illicit.

"Dad?" he asked timidly.

"But…weren't you just downstairs? I saw you downstairs."

"No, Dad. I've been up here about ten minutes. I was watching you in the garden. You looked like you were in deep thought pulling weeds that weren't even there."

Keith said nothing and left. He wondered if he should just go to work instead.

Karl couldn't wait to get out of the house, and Rebecca couldn't blame him. She would have done the same, if she could. But instead, today was going to be the busiest day of her life, and the tension was killing her. With Keith pretending to mess about in the garden, Karl off to a friend's house to spend the day and night (which had actually been a hint on her behalf yesterday), and poor Ashley locked in his bedroom watching movies, she practically had the house to herself. Which was perfect. This way she could speak to Caroline in relative secrecy.

"Yes, she's definitely trying to come back," she said after Caroline asked for the latest update.

"Dear God. I'll be praying for you, Beccy. Are you sure you're ready? You've done everything necessary to send her away once and for all?"

"Yes, I told you. Those graves that were found desecrated; that was me. I took their hearts and ate them while reciting the revocation, basically counteracting what she's done already—her own invocation spell. All I have to do if she appears—*when* she appears—is recite the other one three times, and she will be banished. Before she can get her hands on Ashley."

"Dear Lord. And you're sure it's Ashley she wants, not Karl?"

"Positive. It has to be a firstborn for her to come back. It said so in her own books I found that day. At the stroke of midnight, on the boy's thirteenth birthday, as he enters manhood, is when she can return in full physical form. And, excuse my language, but it's not happening. It's the poor kid's birthday and everyone is moping about like the apocalypse is about to happen. It makes me sick. She makes me sick. It's all my own fault for letting her come and live here. I should have dragged her to Northgate myself."

"You couldn't know, Beccy. None of us could have foreseen this. We all thought it was the ramblings of a madwoman. Lord forgive me, but maybe she should have done a more thorough job when she tried to commit suicide all those years ago."

"The Lord does forgive you. My mother is an abomination. Her place is in Hell, not here. That poor boy was taken from our house, and we can't tell his parents or the police anything. I'm pretty sure the police are still watching us. I keep seeing strange vehicles parked nearby, one's I don't recognise. God help us if anything goes wrong and the detective sees it."

"It will be fine, Beccy, you'll see. God will ensure it."

"Okay. Anyway, I just wanted to let you know that everything is ready. The preparations have been made and, after tonight, we can all get back to normal again. I shall phone you tomorrow. Ashley didn't even want to celebrate his birthday today. He prefers tomorrow, so I'll no doubt see you then. Pray for me, Caroline."

Caroline said she would and hung up.

She thought she would feel better after speaking to Caroline but the dark cloud that had been hanging over her for weeks now, ever since Edna died and Ashley had that first encounter, seemed to grow rather than diminish. It was going to swallow her whole, drain her of all vitality and hope and turn her heart black with terror. She thought of going for a walk, doing some grocery shopping to occupy her thoughts, but the idea of leaving her son alone in the house, albeit with Keith, was something she just couldn't do. It would be like abandoning him to his own fate. Keith had his ideas of what was going on— was almost spot on, in fact—but he wouldn't know how to react should anything occur. It was down to her and her alone. Instead, she went and poured herself a glass of wine and tried dismally to watch a movie on TV. But her concentration levels were so low the film might as well have had the sound turned off or be in Chinese. Slowly, inevitably, the sun began to creep down past the skyline, and its counterpart began to show itself, turning the sky a faded purple. It was almost time.

Keith had mumbled something about having to pop into the office and would be back soon and Karl was gone for the night so for now it was just her and Ashley. She poked her head in and smiled at him in her most reassuring way possible, then went to her bedroom and took out the box hidden at the back of the wardrobe. The revocation spell was in there—not that she needed it. She had memorised the words by heart, but it comforted her to hold it. She headed back downstairs and waited.

As the clock struck eleven and Keith reappeared, looking as terrified as she felt, they heard the first rumblings coming from upstairs. Something heavy was dragging itself across the floor. The dull thuds on the wall, fast then slow, as if tapping Morse code. And then the first of the wails echoed around the house, and they knew it was time.

Chapter

28

Ash knew there was no way he was going to get any sleep. With one eye on the alarm clock beside the bed, he randomly scrolled through Netflix trying to find something, anything, to take his mind off things. Which was impossible. Even his favourite comedy failed to spark a chuckle or even a smile. All he could think about was how Kevin may have met his demise. Was it a slow and painful death, gradually eaten alive by Grandma until nothing remained? Or had it been quick? A snap of the neck, perhaps, to stop him from screaming and alerting others? Is that what Grandma's surprise would be? Somehow, he didn't think so.

After all this time, surely, she wanted to drag it out, make his suffering endure. And this made him wonder what he could possibly have done for her to want to hurt him in the first place. He had always been her favourite. She had told him that very thing in private multiple times. So why this sudden change of heart? He knew from listening to his mother that she had turned senile in her old age, but that was no reason to want to hurt him. And even if she did, and Mum knew about it, why hadn't she done anything, either?

That was another thing. He had howled and begged to stay with them downstairs tonight, so Grandma wouldn't be able to get to him alone. But his mother had insisted he stay in his room and don't move. She would let him know when it was safe to come out. He thought this the worst possible thing he could do as he had woken with Grandma next to him in Karl's bed. It was as if he was making things as easy as possible for her, but Mum insisted. And right now, he desperately needed the toilet. He'd felt like he desperately needed the toilet all day. His intestines were swimming in acid, bile rising to his throat, and he had been on the verge of puking all day through sheer nerves. But now, he really did need that toilet.

He glanced at the clock. It was 11:47. If anything was going to happen, surely it would have by now. His birthday would be over in a few minutes. Maybe Mum had done something to stop Grandma, which meant it was safe to go to the toilet. Mum would be up any second to tell him everything had been fixed, that Grandma was gone forever and tomorrow he could celebrate his birthday and every other one that came after it.

He decided he would be quick, just in case.

Ashley took a deep breath and bolted to the toilet. The relief was immense. He never understood how much a bladder could hold; surely, it must have been bulging against his sides, the size of a balloon. He finished, flushed the chain, and smiled for the first time in days. Ashley opened the bathroom door and turned to close it, hearing the TV on downstairs.

Then he felt a tug at his ankle.

Suddenly, Ashley was on the floor and being dragged by an invisible arm towards the open door of his grandma's room. He screamed—something that was more difficult than he could have imagined because the oxygen had been taken from his lungs. Ashley banged on the carpeted floor when trying to grab onto the staircase or a door frame. He tried to twist himself so he could lash out with his free leg, yet when he did manage to look back, there was nothing there.

He was dragged into the foul-smelling room. The door slammed shut, leaving him in an almost utter darkness. Almost…except for two silvery orbs like far away planets staring down at him. Ashley was aware of yelling, fast, heavy thudding on the stairs and his name being screamed over and over. There were louder thuds, probably his dad trying to kick the door in. Then he heard his mother screaming something unintelligible, over and over. The wardrobe doors opened and a huge, dark figure awaited him with open arms.

The curtains were slightly ajar now, so the full moon was doing its best to make sure Ashley could see his fate and what awaited him. His grandma stood there, a semi-translucent figure, the greying flesh wobbling on her great bulk as she swayed. Her mouth opened into a cavernous black pit that would swallow him whole. Her arms, like huge dead branches, outstretched for him, fingers curled into wicked talons that would tear his head off. Strands of grey hair blew from a sudden wind that had picked up, like old cobwebs waving in the breeze. And then he was dragged closer to the wardrobe, its doors wide open, as though welcoming him. He grunted as he was dragged over the bottom of the wardrobe and his legs disappeared into the abyss.

"Happy birthday!" came a wheezed, husky voice. "Grandma told you she had a surprise for you. I'm your surprise, little one. We're going to live forever, me and you together. Isn't that sweet? I said I loved you, didn't I? I'm going to love you forever and forever. You will be a part of me, and we will live joined eternally."

She cackled then, the hoarse shriek of an old crow, and he was taken further into the wardrobe, just his arms and torso sticking out.

"Mum! Dad! Help! Grandma's gonna eat me. Please help!"

It sounded like a battering ram was being driven repeatedly into the bedroom door. His mother was screaming and howling and maybe she had gone mad, too, because she kept repeating the same words again and again in a language he didn't know. But the door wouldn't budge. And then he was fully inside the wardrobe now and one of his questions was finally answered. There on the floor lay the pyjamas Kevin had been wearing the night he disappeared, crumpled in a heap and covered in blood.

"Please, Grandma, don't. Don't hurt me. I haven't done anything wrong."

She cackled again, a diseased, sick crony who seemed to find his pathetic whimpering funny and amusing.

"You didn't have to do anything wrong. All you had to do was be born—my firstborn. And now we are finally together, and we can go find my beloved Alison at last."

Two huge, flabby arms reached down and picked him up, just as the bedroom door was finally kicked in. He looked up into the face of a monster, an undead creature come back from the dead with its glowing, hungry eyes and wide, bottomless pit of a mouth. She was going to eat him alive, after all— another question answered. Her tongue licked scabby, raw lips, greying teeth like tombstones gnashing together in anticipation as they drew closer and closer to his face, her breath that of a long-dead thing.

"Ash! No!" came his dad's voice, but it was too late.

"Edna, you let him be; I command thee!" came his mother's voice. "Return to your grave; I command thee. Be gone!"

She cackled again, seemingly ignorant of her daughter's revocation spell.

Ashley tried to wriggle free from her tight grip, still confident his mother would hold true to her promise. She had to; her promise was golden. And yet, as the wardrobe doors began to close, despite Keith doing everything he could to stop it from happening, Ashley's hope faded as fast as the weak light still present in the room.

The last thing he heard as jaws clamped firmly yet softly around his throat was his parent's frantic screams for Grandma to leave him alone and return him to them and both of them banging and kicking on the wardrobe doors, so loud it was like a bomb going off. The last thing he felt was his grandma's sticky, wet tongue on his face. Then the world went completely dark, Edna's warm breath flooding his nostrils, her promise of eternity reverberating in his dying head.

Grandma's cold, clammy flesh smothered him into a hug for the very last time.

Chapter

29

"To be honest, you're going to have to come up with something better that," said Detective Riddley. "If we add up the evidence, we have your husband attempting to dig up your mother's grave, your son's friend missing, and now your own son has disappeared as well. Something doesn't add up, Mrs. Rice. To me, it screams of some child sex ring, or even a satanic cult or something. It also makes me worry about your other son. Children just don't disappear like that in the middle of the night, with no one seeing or hearing them taken from their own bedrooms. You can expect a lot more visits from us, so you better start thinking about what really happened if you don't want to see your other son put in a foster home."

Karl listened to the conversation from behind the living room door. His mother said nothing. She hadn't said a word since Ashley disappeared. Neither had his dad. They seemed to be in some kind of permanent daze, the only sounds their crying when

they thought Karl wasn't listening. But he was
listening.

He was always listening.

He quickly scurried away when he heard the
detective get up and announce he was leaving. His
mother followed him, opened the door, and watched
him leave after another exchange of words. She closed
the door softly, stared at the floor for a while, then
shuffled back to the sofa. Karl wasn't entirely sure
what had happened. He had heard things, and he knew
that Ashley had been scared of Grandma, which was
weird because she was dead. So what did he have to be
scared of? Could it be true that people really did come
back from the dead like some of the horror movies he
had sneaked a look at on the internet? Ashley had
always told him monsters didn't exist; they were just
figments of people's imagination. Whatever a figment
was.

He had cried a lot himself in the days following
Ashley's disappearance. He couldn't believe it had
happened; something about being kidnapped while
Mum and Dad were asleep in bed. That's what they
told him and the police, anyway. But it seemed
impossible. Maybe it was going to happen to Karl as
well, but again, things didn't make sense. Either
Grandma was dead and Ashley had been kidnapped or
they hadn't; it had to be one or the other, So why
would his parents lie?

The police had been to their home a lot in the last few days, demanding to search the whole house. Even Grandma's old room, which wasn't locked anymore. Karl had been in there himself several times, and it was completely empty; no bed, wardrobe or anything. So why all the fuss about staying out, he didn't know. There were lots of things he didn't know lately.

Some he thought he did, though.

What he thought was that for some reason Mum and Dad were lying about Ashley's whereabouts and Grandma being dead. Because, despite what his parents had told him about bad dreams and nightmares, then something about the mind playing funny tricks, he knew this wasn't true. He asked a teacher at school, and Mrs. Collins said that in dreams smells didn't exist. That was how he knew for sure it was all real. Because when Ashley and Grandma came to visit him at night, when he was in bed, they smelled disgusting.

Thank you for enjoying book TWO of the Creepy Little Nightmare series.

Justin Boote is an Englishman who has been living in Barcelona for the last 30 years and has been writing for the last 6. He started off writing short stories for various anthologies and magazines. To date, around 50 of the 200+ short stories he has written have been published, including 15 in the highly popular Night Terrors series by Scare Street.

Since turning to novels in 2021 when Covid forced his workplace to close down permanently, he has written and published eleven novels and three short story collections. He lives with his wife, son, and cat, who each take turns trying to disrupt him from his new lifestyle and failing dismally with the possible exception of Fat Cat.

Made in the USA
Middletown, DE
26 December 2022

20395069R00154